Mr.Right

A journey towards him

Shweta Brijpuria

FROG BOOKS

ISBN 978-93-52017-46-1

First published in India in 2016 by Frog Books
An imprint of Leadstart Publishing Pvt. Ltd.

Sales Office:
Unit No. 25-26, Building No. A/1,
Near Wadala RTO,
Wadala (East), Mumbai – 400037, India
Phone: +91 96 99933000
Email: info@leadstartcorp.com
www.leadstartcorp.com

US Office:
Axis Corp, 7845 E, Oakbrook Circle,
Madison, WI 53717, USA

Editor: Shruti Bhiwandiwala
Cover: Nishant
Layouts: Chandravadan Ramchandra Shiroorkar

Typeset in Palatino Linotype
Printed at Repro

Dedication

Mr Right is dedicated to all women who believe in walking down a journey towards their Mr. Right and guys who become their strength. It is the power of togetherness that drives a happy life. An uncompromising spirit of believing in yourself and living with the love that you choose.

This book is dedicated to all the parents and their undying efforts to get the right match for their daughter.

I dedicate this book to my Mr Right, for his love and support all through our journey, my parents who believe in me, my teachers who inspired me to write, my friends, my publisher, readers who appreciate my work..

ABOUT THE AUTHOR

A poet at heart and marketer by profession, Shweta Brijpuria is a hard core Bhopali. As eldest sibling in her family, she enjoys the role of 'didi' even outside home. She is known in the family for doing things she once feared.

Having worked as a marketer with many brands, she believes the first step towards creating something is to believe in one's ability to create and then working towards it. People travel places; she travels brands, connects with them, nurtures them and grows with them.

Acknowledgements

The journey towards Mr Right is long. While Nisha was finding hers, I was walking towards mine. I would like to thank everyone who played an important role in both Nisha and my journey.

I would like to thank my parents for standing tall while I took the most challenging decision of my life. Thank you Kavita Maa, you are a wonderful person.

My brothers Deepak, Chirag, Saurabh, Vaibahv and sisters Niti and Vibhooti have always been my inspiration and given me the reason to keep going on.

Satish, my Mr Right, whom I have known for around 12 years now. We walked a journey where our role for each other kept changing. At every new stage we discovered a new reason to connect stronger. Never realised when we became 'us'. Thank you for the lovely friendship we share.

Thank you Davina, Varsha, Tina, Yash, Malini, Uzair and Amrita for your patience throughout Nisha's search for her Mr Right. She could have never met the perfect one without your support.

I would like to thank all bookstores for the love and support given to Dark White. Thank you Indurji,

Salimji, Manoharji, Walid and entire Leadstart team for your support in marketing of Dark White and showing confidence in Nisha and her Mr Right. Thanks team Redwall Media works for online support given to Dark White. Would like to thank all the readers of Dark White, your love encouraged me to write this book and I am sure Mr Right would receive the same love.

Whatsapp and Facebook have connected us again. I would like to thank all my school, college friends and teachers. Thanks to all my friends from work and outside work.

Thanks to media friends for all the love and encouragement. Thank you critics for your encouraging feedback. It is indeed a motivation to keep going on.

It is an awesome life and you all have made it one for me.

Prologue

"Can we take a photo, Vikram?" I asked, as we left the dinner table.

He smirked and said, "A photo...why? Don't you want to meet me again?"

I looked at him, gave him my most convincing smile and said, "Vikram, I don't meet nice people every day, when I do, I like to capture the moment."

He stared at me for a few minutes. I knew he was trying to figure out what I was up to. He was too smart to fall for that trite reply, but I remained silent, hoping that he would agree to my request.

Luckily, he agreed and we took our photograph. As I looked at the photograph, I thought to myself. *We look like friends, good friends, but nothing more. He is a nice, handsome and smart man with a successful career. He likes travelling, reading, sports and music. We have so much in common, yet I know he is not the one for me. The time we spent talking over the phone and at dinner had reaffirmed my decision. We are not meant to be. We are too similar. We are both set in our ways and settled in our careers. Most important, neither of us want to change. We will make wonderful friends, but not great lifelong companions. The only thing left was to tell him. The only question was how?*

Normally, rejecting a proposal is easy. I tell Mom that I did not like the guy and she passes on the information to his parents. Or the guy passes on the information to his parents and they inform my mother, making the process much simpler. This time it was different. Vikram had become a friend. I did not want to hurt him, nor did I want to insult him by informing about my decision through a third person.

How do I tell him that I do not want to marry him? Should I be blunt? Should I cushion the news? Which approach would be less painful?

In the midst of my mental chaos, Vikram's voice broke through.

"Would you like to go for a walk with me?"

I smiled and immediately agreed, hoping to find a right moment to break the news without hurting him.

As we walked down the path, I began to shiver. The weather was cold and there was a strong breeze. I forgot my jacket at home, since it was hot when I left home. Before I could complain or ask to move to a less breezy spot, I felt like I had been transported into a romantic scene from a Hindi movie, as Vikram took off his jacket and draped it around my shoulders.

I froze. I looked at the jacket, then I looked at him and promptly burst into laughter.

He gave me a big broad grin and said, "I bet you didn't expect that."

I definitely did not. Little things like these had made him a good friend. I wish I felt more, and did not have to hurt him by telling that I don't see him as a lifelong companion.

"Thank you, Vikram," I pause, "We need to talk," before I could say another word, he cut me off.

Damn it! He is not going to propose, is he? He was just being a gentleman not romantic - wasn't he?

I looked at him, trying not to react without hearing what he had to say.

He smiled at me gently and said, "Nisha, I know what you are going to say. We are not right for each other. I hope we can be friends and in a few months meet up again with our respective Mr and Mrs Right."

I smiled, we agreed and went our separate ways.

Chapter 1

Monday. Time to get away from the chaos of marriage mart and get back to the grind of work.

As I walk into the office, I could hear loud voices. This does not surprise me. The Bijal Group is a unique company with a strong work culture that includes conducting discussions at high volumes. The day I walk into a quiet office is the day I will worry.

I avoid the arguing horde and step into the cafeteria, hoping to grab a cup of coffee and unearth the cause of today's drama.

As I enter, I hear colleagues from a different department talking.

"Desai Sahab, I received a call at 4:30 in the morning, my wife asked me not to disturb her sleep, and sit in the balcony to continue my conversation."

"That's normal, Singh Sahab, if you don't pick up a call you realise that a delay of an hour or two can cause much chaos but answering the call leads to personal chaos."

"Production is a tough business, Desai Sahab. My daughter says she will not marry any guy from our field."

I could not help but laugh. It seems like work and marriage are the two big issues in everyone's life. I enquire about their health and head to my cabin to begin my day.

As I enter, I cannot help but smile. It is a large cabin, bigger than cabins allotted to some of the seniors. It has a huge window, cute light pink walls, lovely artwork and matching furniture. It looks like a picture from an interior design magazine. Best of all, my name and designation are boldly embossed on the glass door. Nisha Chandra - Project General Manager. This cabin is a symbol of my growth. I started at the Bijal Group as a fresh college graduate and now a General Manager on the path to becoming VP. Ironically, I nearly did not get the job due to a clerical error.

Eight years ago, I had an interview with the company's MD. I was nervous, it was my first interview and I was far from home. My nerves became worse as soon as I walked through the door, realising I had somehow created a negative impression instantly. The MD, Mr Bijal did not smile or acknowledge my squeaky 'good morning', he just glared at me and without any introduction started abruptly with his list of technical questions. I answered them one by one but still found him dissatisfied. I could not help but wonder what was off-putting about me. Was my hair untidy? Did I smell after travelling for hours in the hot sun? Maybe my educational background caused the MD to look at me with such disdain. I had graduated from NRIT—a regional college, an A-level college, but far less impressive when compared to his—IIT Mumbai.

As the interview proceeded, I began to get depressed. Despite my efforts to be cheerful and smart, I was aware that he found me lacking. Perversely, as we spoke, I could not help but be impressed. I was well grounded in engineering knowledge and terminologies, but this man had started a unique company that created construction equipment for buildings. I wanted to be part of this company—if only I could figure out what I had done wrong.

"Ms Poornima," he began to dismiss me.

I immediately stopped him and informed that my name is Nisha Chandra. He looked at me quizzically as I handed him my resume. He looked at the resume, pulled out a calculator and asked me to wait outside. Thoroughly confused, I stepped outside trying to understand what the hell happened. Ten minutes later, I was ecstatic and even more bewildered. Despite the rotten interview, I had been offered my dream position at the Bijal Group.

A few weeks later, I finally understood what had gone on during my interview. It turned out that Mr Bijal, my Sindhi boss, is a great believer in numerology. He believes that to be successful, you not only have to work hard, but also hire people with the right numerological background. His disinterest in me wasn't because I lacked the right qualification; it was because the missing Ms. Poornima didn't have the right numerological background which he was looking for. He sent me out and asked to wait because he wanted to calculate my numerology number, match it with his and the company's number, which was based on our combined birth and inception dates. Ms. Poornima's birth date did not match his requirements. Thankfully, mine did!

I had to work really hard to prove my merit against the label that I received after this numerology factor playing a crucial role in my selection at Bijals. Everybody used to look at me as a person from some other planet.

Anyways ....enough reminiscing, time to work!

After a busy day at work, I head home to Silven Heights in Lower Parel, not even a thirty-minute drive from the office. I lived as a paying guest in Mira Road, when I had just moved to Mumbai as a young project trainee. Every day was a struggle, travelling in the crowded local trains to reach office at the other end of the city and then travelling back home, dealing with the same crowd. Over the years, I moved closer to office and even purchased a car. One good aspect of all my moving around from Mira Road to Lower Parel was the increasing familiarity with the city. Unlike eight years ago, I am no longer a timid, young girl afraid of the big city, easily lost and easily scared.

I walk into my house to the sound of blaring music. My flatmate, Karishma, must be stressed again. I really do not know why she cannot meditate to gain peace of mind. Every time I ask her, the answer is same.

"Nisha, I am a lawyer. I work for a big law firm. Partners in the company picked us, trained us and expect us to defend whoever pays for our services whether they are innocent or guilty. The objective is to uphold the firm's name not be a moral compass. Dwelling on my inner self is not conducive to career growth."

Pointless as the conversation may be, I should try to calm her down. I really don't want to deal with irate neighbours again, complaining about the volume of music.

"Hey, Karishma, how is work?" I get a glare in reply.

"I don't know why you do this to yourself, Karishma."

"I am a successful lawyer Nisha."

"So you are willing to undergo mental torture to be successful?"

"Yes, I am!"

"You hate working for this Firm, Karishma."

"Yes, I do," she looks at me in the eye with a serious expression on her face and says, "but for you, tomorrow, I will go to the office, resign, buy a table, chair and an umbrella, set up my own practice outside the High Court and meditate daily."

We both burst out laughing, knowing that will never happen.

I don't know why I try. I know she is not going to change. She is a firm believer in the philosophy - Meditating requires concentration and reflection, but going to the gym only requires physical effort, so let's exercise.

That does not seem like a very smart philosophy to me. How do you expect peace of mind if you only work on your body and not on your mind?

But then most her philosophies are strange.

She married, divorced and had an affair with the same man. They still go out to party together. They just don't want to be married. They have a daughter who lives in a hostel during the school year and at her grandparents' homes during the school break. Neither set of grandparents is willing to trust the couple with their only grandchild. In a world, where most mothers will do anything for their children, Karishma is an oddity who just wants to live free.

Karishma's quirks and foibles make her an interesting person in my life, but it does add drama to my already complicated personal life. My mother absolutely hates her. I am certain that she sees Karishma as the root of all evil. She believes that Karishma's life has coloured my perspective towards marriage. In fact, she is certain that Karishma is a bad influence who will convince me to never marry. She doesn't know that there are other factors involved.

Speaking of my mother, it is surprising she hasn't called yet to inquire if she should finally start planning my wedding with Vikram.

I know I should be grateful that my family lives in Nagpur and I only have to deal with phone calls, nagging me about getting married.

In the past two years, I have met 17 men.

17!

The only thing I have gotten out of those meetings is enough content to write a book. Some of those meetings were disastrous, others funny. Some had unique "proposal" stories. Vikram was number 18. He, at least, was smart and could carry a conversation. Too bad, we weren't right for each other, then I wouldn't have to tell my mother that this proposal hadn't worked out.

Wait! What if?

A smirk spread across my face as I sent my mother the photograph from last night with the caption 'Vikram and Nisha —Friends Forever'.

Now I will not have to deal with 'that' awkward conversation until she brings up the next irritating soul on her never-ending prospective son-in-law list.

Chapter 2

The next few days pass by quickly and quietly. I woke up, headed to the gym, went to work and came home. There are no changes in my routine. My mother had not called since my message, I didn't know whether to be worried or to be pleased.

Work has been going well. I completed one more project well ahead of the deadline. My company will receive a bonus and I am hoping that the senior management will look at my efforts and reward me not only monetarily but with a promotion as well. One day soon, I hope to be the Vice President of the Technical Division. I know my scorecard will take me there. In the last eight years, my graph has shown a remarkable growth and everyone has acknowledged that, despite the numerology factor.

As I head to work, I cannot help but reflect on my own life and philosophies. I live a balanced life irrespective of worldly approvals. My weekends are full - either networking with social groups to build contacts or going to the movies with friends. Romantic Hindi movies are my weakness. I always hope that my Mr. Right is as perfect for me as Raj is for Simran in *DDLJ*.During the week, work consumes my time.

I freely admit that I am workaholic and I know my belief that travel is torture and work is bliss makes my days begin earlier than most people. I leave before eight and come home late, to avoid the traffic. Instead of an average eight-hour workday, I work 12 to13 hours. But I do make sure my day starts right by travelling alone and listening to music.

As I enter the office, I am greeted with a message to head to the MD's office as soon as possible.

I can't help but worry. Why does he want to speak to me so urgently? Am I in trouble? Were my designs rejected by the client? I worked so hard on this project for the last three months. I met with the architect almost every other day. I forced myself to endure his company, despite his constant flatulence after meals, to ensure the project was perfect. After all that effort, if this project is rejected, I will kill him.

After keeping my bag in the cabin, I try to compose myself before heading to Mr Bijal's office.

I enter his cabin and greet him with a bright 'good morning' hoping to gauge his mood and the news.

I look at his face and my heart stops. He is not wearing his glasses. The glasses only came off when his anger reaches a peak and he is about to raise his voice. I do not want to be the target of his anger early in the morning, nor do I want to lose my temper.

Not that I cannot manage his anger, I learnt early on how to deal with angry superious. Interestingly, now that I am older and at a higher position, I find myself learning tricks to handle juniors. It's almost an art of living at different career stages.

I better pay attention, if I want to counter his anger. His glasses are off, yet he is so composed, there must be some other trick.

I look closely, he isn't angry. I relax and gamely start the conversation in Gujju-style, "*Kem cho*, Sir."

"Nisha, come and sit down, we need to have a serious discussion."

"Sir, did something happen?"

"I am happy to inform you that the management is considering promoting you to Vice President, awarding you for your efforts and excellent results."

"Thank you, Sir, I am so excited and grateful."

"Wait, Nisha. Before you get too excited, you need to understand this position is not yet yours. While you are capable, you are still very young and you will have to prove to the management that you have what it takes."

This statement takes away the excitement and leaves behind anger.

"Sir, I have proven myself, and my scorecard is clearly an indication of my capability. In just seven years, I have climbed from simple project intern to the general manager. You have challenged and encouraged me to strive for better and better. Why do you doubt my capability now?" I said almost everything that came to my mind without even considering the repercussions my words would create. I just got carried away. This is where I fail when it comes to dealing with people.

"Nisha, we don't doubt your ability to do the work, what we worry about is your ability to manage. You are extremely capable and that is why we want to offer you this position, but we are also aware you are young and extremely emotional. We need to be sure that you can manage the pressure in a befitting manner."

"Sir, I know how to do my job. You won't find anyone better."

"No, Nisha, you know how to do your current job. You don't know how to be a VP. Currently, you only have to come up with designs and hand down instructions. You do not look at the bigger picture. At the VP level, you will have to give up your attachment to the design and technical work. You will have to leave them to the designers and technicians while focusing on the bigger picture."

"What does that mean Sir?"

"Nisha, you have to look at how each decision you make, affects not only your project, but also the rest of the company. You have to analyse which project will draw in the most rewards, which will benefit the company most. You can no longer limit your focus to a single project; you have to look after the complete business unit.

A brilliant example is Kabir. I know you don't like me praising Kabir, but his skills and strategies have strengthened the company in a short period of time.

Eight years ago, we could only boast that we have introduced one new brilliant piece of technology in India. Kabir's strategic planning has helped us become the company, which has developed and produced the maximum innovative products in the industry. We have even started to export. Now our clients use our brand as a reference to promote their projects."

"Sir, you want me to think and act like Kabir?"

"Nisha, I am just giving you an example. He is a capable VP and deserves respect for his skills and strategy. Whether or not you like him personally should not change the way you treat him professionally. This attitude of yours is the reason behind our doubts. You need to decide whether you are capable of treating every person fairly, whether you like them personally or not."

"OK, Sir, I think I understand what you mean."

I get up to leave, unable to stomach any more speeches about the greatness of Kabir and my character flaws.

"Nisha, just one more piece of advice. We have worked together for many years. I have watched with pride as you have grown from a fresher to General Manager. I have guided you on your journey. At times, I almost feel like your father. Your dedication is commendable and I want you to succeed, but before you can, you will have to mature. You can no longer afford to have a 'my on- time delivery gave the company good profits' - attitude.

You have to be able to draw the entire road map—what profitable projects to take up, the revenue they would generate, when, what resources to put in these projects and in how much time to complete these projects. If you get the VP position, you will be the profit centre head.

So, please broaden your vision. Don't let the past prevent you from succeeding. Spend the next few months observing Kabir. Let him train you. With his help, you are sure to succeed."

"Sir, training with Kabir has never helped me. You placed me under him when I started and that was a disaster. Whatever I learnt, whatever I have achieved, is all without his help. I came this far without him, and I can achieve the next step without him too."

"I expect better from you, Nisha."

I could hear the disappointment in his tone and see the displeasure on his face. It struck to me that I had made a blunder. I wanted to take back my words.

Why? Why? Every time Kabir crops up, I lose my mind. I hate the person I become. Now my bluntness towards the man he respects could cost me my promotion and Mr Bijal's respect.

"Sir, I did not mean it like that," I say, trying to cover up my blunder.

"Then what do you mean?" he asks.

"Sir, Kabir became VP of his division just four years ago while my efforts brought me to this position in just 8 years of my career. Does it not prove that I am better than him and need no training from him? When I take charge of this position, I might get more profits to the company."

"Nisha, he was considered for the VP position in just six years of his career, but we didn't have an available position or the capacity to accommodate him, then. The job he has, was created especially for him due to his outstanding performance. As far as you are concerned, your name is just proposed, nothing has been finalised."

"Sir...." I try to say something and he stops me.

"Nisha I repeat it's this attitude that creates doubts about whether you are capable or worthy of the VP position. If you cannot handle old personal issues gracefully, then how will you tactfully and diplomatically handle strategic issues? As a VP, you will have to deal with Kabir and his department on a daily basis, but with this attitude, I am sorry, we cannot take the risk of giving you that responsibility."

It is getting too much. Just because he has generated business does not mean that others are incapable and that too without being given a chance. I have generated much profit and recognition for the company with my accuracy and on-time delivery of projects, but he is not considering that at all.

"Sir, trust me, I will not beg for any position, if I deserve it, surely will get it. Trust me it will be Kabir who will have to deal with my department, not me."

"Nisha, you need to re-evaluate your attitude. Please leave before you say something that you will regret. Keep in mind, the decision is still to be made."

"Yes, Sir, I will keep that in mind."

As I leave the room, I knew I would not get any work done so decide to head home. I get into the car and drive faster than usual. My mind refuses to switch off, I cannot believe Mr Bijal would say something like this. My efforts clearly have no value.

I have put my heart and soul into this company. I have worked hard to complete projects not only on time, but ahead of schedule. Despite crises no project of mine has incurred penalties. After all that hard work, my efforts are not appreciated.

I deserve the VP position. I have proven my capability.

But no! I'm too emotional. Why doesn't he realise that my emotions drive me? My emotions have helped me reach this position.

To make matters worse, to get what I deserve, I will have to follow Kabir S. Singh around like a puppy.

Why Kabir S. Singh? There are other VPs at Bijal Group. But no! I have to train with Kabir S. Singh, the shrewd, corporate whale with no emotions.

Just talking about him spoils my day. I don't like his existence neither in the office nor anywhere else in my life.

I hate that the Board has been dissecting my life.

****

Driving home, I meet with a small accident. I try to rest when home, but that does not calm the chaos in my mind. To divert the disturbing thoughts, I call mother.

This is how VPs' act, when stress reaches its peak, shamelessly create stakeholders, make them feel responsible for the stress and pass on the burden.

My Mother

"Mom, I banged my car."

"So what, Nisha, I bang the car every other day."

"Mom, you bang Papa's car, I banged my car."

"Nisha *beta*, had I banged yours, my answer would still have been the same. As long as you are fine, it does not matter."

"Mom, I thought you would understand, but you decide to be silly. Sometimes I really wonder whether you are my mother."

"Nisha, you feel that way only because you don't understand the true worry. A dent on your car does not matter, you being unmarried matters. You should have been married by now and the person you should have called after an accident should have been your husband, not me."

"Mom, you are going to drive me crazy. Why are you speaking nonsense?"

"Nonsense! At your age, your mother should not be the most important person in your life. You are ruining your life."

"Mom, I cannot talk to you. Where's Papa?"

"He's travelling. You can't speak to him, his phone is out of coverage."

"OK, Mom, I am going to sleep before you get me so stressed that I get a heart attack."

"Me? Give you a heart attack? Nisha, you will give us heart attack with your refusal to marry. We have given you too much freedom. Go talk to your friends for life."

"Bye, Mom! I will talk to you when you are not insane."

My mother, the drama queen! I hoped that by sending her the picture I would avoid a lengthy and painful discussion on why Vikram wasn't the one. I had hoped she would accept the situation easily and move on quickly. But no, she remembers every detail and throws it in my face at the most inappropriate time.

As it is I was stressed because of work and the accident, but no, she will not stop forcing me to get married.

It is not like I don't want to get married. I just do not want to marry any of the jokers they keep pushing my way.

All I asked was a few years' time to build a career. I did not want a life at the mercy of a man. But no, they wouldn't agree. Papa kept pushing me to meet prospects since my last semester in college. They wanted me to get married immediately after my exams.

Every new joker I meet makes me happy that I took my life's decision in my hand, lied to them about the project, came to Mumbai for the interview at Bijal Group and bagged the job in the first round itself.

I know my act was very impulsive, had it been me in their place there would have been no room for communication, even if it was the daughter of the family. Kabir made one wrong move and now has come into the list of most unwanted people in my life, despite being my life at one point of time.

Chapter 3

Life has been pretty simple, except for the times when my parents make it difficult by sending these jokers along my way.

First it was Ravi. I met him when he along with his family came to my home in Nagpur.

Ravi's family was well off, with a grain trading business. They had been looking for a perfect *bahu* for their beloved son, for quite some time. This process had been a prolonged one, as his sister had rejected 500 girls as not worthy of her brother. My family was determined that 501 would be the lucky number. It wasn't about me marrying the right man, it was the prestige of being selected over all the rejected ones.

To please my family, I was on my best behaviour. I smiled sweetly, acted innocent and did not make any sarcastic remarks, even when they were rude. I was determined to be at my best, while ensuring that they lose the game.

I was happy when I heard my signal to prove that it was the guy's calibre that was questionable, not any of those 500 girls.

"*Beta* Nisha, we have asked all the questions we wanted.

Chandra*ji*, we like your daughter. If Nisha has any questions she can ask."

Everyone looked at me. Papa looked at me, giving a hint that I am not supposed to ask anything. Mom was a little taken aback.

I smiled. I was going to ask my questions. I didn't want to belong to a family that thought bragging about insulting 500 girls was a great achievement.

I looked down, acted shy and asked for an interactive session. Very politely, I looked at Ravi, who suddenly looked a bit uncomfortable as did the others.

"So, you stay abroad?"

"Yes," he replied.

"For how many years now?"

"Almost ten."

"No girlfriend?"

He almost spilt the coffee from his cup. He did not expect this question from a shy, sweet girl who had passed his tests.

I faked an apology, "I hope I am not asking you anything that is not normal for a guy staying abroad."

With extreme politeness, he replied, "Yes, I had three girlfriends in the past."

"Oh, they left you?"

"It was kind of a mutual break-up with all of them."

"Is it that difficult to stay with you?"

To this, he gave me an enraged look, rudely handed over his cup of coffee to me, signalled his family and drove off.

If this incident wasn't bad enough, then there was the meeting with Shashank's sister. She and her husband had a stopover in Mumbai and I met them at the airport so that she could give the family a green signal for Shashank and me to meet.

Amusing, isn't it? We are both adults, but our parents' decide if we are suitable for each other and it is his little sister who decides whether we meet or not.

I worry about these meetings with sisters, who despite being married have such strong say in the lives of their brothers. I am always worried that I will not be able to deal with them.

Despite my concerns, I went to meet her. Papa gave me her husband Amit's, number and expected me to call him to fix a meeting.

Now just imagine, you are given a strange guy's number who is someone else husband and you are expected to call and arrange for a meeting with him.

It's awkward.

Still, I did as asked.

The couple was very nice and I even liked them but as I reached home, there was a call from papa saying that the girl was complaining about me and about my *mehemaan navaazi*.

Then came the shocker that I insulted her and her husband by not calling them Sapna*ji* and Amit*ji* or *Jiji* and *Jijaji*. I was amazed. These two people with whom I spent sixty minutes weren't shy of expressing their love for each other in the most modern way possible.

I don't even know when, during those sixty minutes, they became my *Jiji* and *Jijaji* so much so that my not calling that offended them. Above that, how was me not calling them '*ji*' rude? It was a meeting to decide whether I should meet Shashank or not and not to please them.

It was too much to take. After getting that needless firing from Papa, I immediately called Amit to ask him - if he wanted to be called '*ji*', why he didn't mention in those sixty minutes.

To my surprise he shifted the entire blame on his beloved wife. It was strange to see the 'much-in-love' newlywed modern couple playing blame games in just one month of marriage.

Thankfully, she apologised to my parents for the ruckus she created, but I no longer wanted to do anything with that family.

And let's not forget about the proposal from my second cousin's family.

Three years ago, mom insisted I meet Amol, as they wanted me to marry him to revive old family relations. They had this ridiculous idea that Amol and I would get married and post-marriage they would change my name to that of my grandmother's name so that the daughter they gave away to Chandras would return home.

Post-marriage, I was expected to move my base from Mumbai to a small village, and not another metropolitan.

I would have to live in an ancestral house, which was over 100 years old, built by my father's maternal grandfather, a farmer.

The architecture was beautiful, but the house was falling apart. It had never been renovated and it would never be, since it was a heritage building. I would have not been allowed to pursue my career, in fact, the only acceptable work would have been house chores. This would be my life, after spending years to earn my degree from one of the best engineering colleges and working as a project manager (my designation at the time) for a company that makes advanced technology products for constructing houses.

Thank God! They demanded dowry - they wanted a complete deal, the daughter of the family and all the gold they gave to her, three generations back. If they hadn't, I would have been trapped in a frame of a village woman whose job was to clean the house balcony with cow dung.

There definitely was logic in their proposal, but unfortunately the timing was wrong. This is a different era. Dowry is a crime – Period.

I do not want to live like Karishma, but does my family really expect me to embrace such insanity? I am a well-educated young woman with a successful career and they expect me to give up everything I have worked for to become a housewife in a tiny, obscure village.

The drama behind the prospects they choose for me is so astonishing that I find myself facing a new challenge with every new person. It does not come as a process, but a new stage all together, where sometimes I get life-lines, while other times I get into trouble, but I surely graduate to the next level.

They think I'm too independent and choosy but I am definitely not going to accept such ridiculous proposals.

Thankfully, so far I have been able to play Mom and Papa against each other to escape marrying the many weird men they have introduced into my life as potential life partners.

I think it is time to take an off from work and get rid of the stress. Tomorrow will be a perfect day for it! I should go for a drive.

Chapter 4

People usually start their morning with an alarm clock to wake, I don't need one. My mother calls at the break of day.

"Good morning, Mom."

"Good morning, Nishu. I hope you are feeling better since your accident. Where were you yesterday? I tried calling you multiple times."

I smile. I can never stay mad at Mom for very long. She drives me crazy with her never-ending parade of men, but she does love me a lot and I have never doubted that.

"I am fine, Mom. I went on a long drive yesterday and forgot my phone at home. By the time I came back, it was late and didn't want to disturb you. Why were you calling?"

"But you met an accident just a day before?"

"Mom, I am fine. Do not act worried now. The concern was needed when I called you the other day."

"Behave yourself, Nishu."

"Sorry. How are you?"

"Nisha, I have a good news."

I sigh. Not another guy please! It hasn't been even three weeks since the last one. How does she find them so quickly?

I better play along or I will be forced to listen to a long lecture first thing in the morning.

"Yes, Mom. What's this good news?"

"A nice Mumbai boy is going to call you today. Speak to him nicely and try not to make him your friend for life or I will never have a son-in-law for life. I am tired of going to your friend's and their siblings weddings with gifts and envelopes; I would like to see them at your wedding now."

Oh no, another story to add to my never-ending collection.

"Mom, did you call me early in the morning to complain that you don't want to attend marriages of people and give gifts. Instead you want them to return whatever you gave."

"Don't put words in my mouth, Nishu. I am not complaining about giving gifts. All I want is that people should come to my house for my daughter's wedding."

"Yeah, and return all the gifts and envelopes that you had given to them," I say jokingly, hoping to ease the tension.

"Why don't you understand, Nishu?"

"No worries, Maa. I will talk to your Mumbai guy, what does he do?"

"Oh, I don't know. I have stopped asking that question."

"Oh my God! Are you just handing out my phone number to random strangers now? Aren't you worried that they could be unemployed or dangerous? Do you really want a killer for a son-in-law or a drunkard who cannot support me or our children?"

"Nisha, don't be so dramatic. There is no need to worry. We run background checks and talk to the parents before sending them your number. We know that you are mature enough to handle difficult people."

Oh, the irony, my overdramatic mother asks me not be dramatic.

"Oh please, Mom, I hope you are joking! I will talk to you later as I refuse to let you spoil my day. Bye!"

"I don't mind doing that, I only want my happiness." No one in this world can be as self-centred as my mother.

"Mom, you should want your daughter's happiness and not yours, that's how most mothers are."

"Oh please, Nishu, your happiness is the same as mine. You and your father are always ready to argue. The only thing I am scared of is the amount of time in hand. Everything you have done in the past makes it so difficult to trust you. You don't realise that you are making your own life difficult. I know what is right for you. Bye."

I love my mother. She may talk a lot and lose the essence of the conversation, but she is modest enough to tell you where you are wrong. She is determined, if she wants to boast about something, she does not make things up, instead she convinces the rest of us to work towards her goal and slog until she can truthfully boast about it. It's funny, but we love her anyway.

I will talk to her Mumbai guy. My mother will be happy and who knows, '19' may prove to be the lucky number.

I better move it or else I will be late to work. Now what do I wear? Hmm, I think red will be colour of the day. Shall wear my red dress, red shoes, carry red bag and apply red make up. I am sure that will intrigue Shrija. She is the only one at work who knows that my clothes reflect my mood and I only wear red when I am happy.

I bet she will ask me the reason for red, the moment she sees me.

Just as I predicted, I barely started working when Shrija comes to my cabin.

"Hey, what's up, babe?"

"Hi, Shrija. All good. So you are early today."

"No, you are on normal office time today. So what is the reason behind the red?"

"Oh yes, didn't realise it's me who is late today, well yesterday was..."

My cell phone begins to ring, interrupting our conversation. It is an unknown number, I look at it and sigh!

"Shrija, give me a few minutes, will you? I have to take this call else my mother will be the one calling in anger."

As I answer the call a heavy voice greets me from the other side, seems like a bodybuilder on the other side.

"Hi, Nisha, I am Mahesh, your mother shared your number. Is this a good time to talk?"

"Hi, Mahesh, can we talk in the evening? It is a little difficult to speak during the office hours."

"Sure, Ma'am, no problem. Just drop me a message when you are home." It is funny when you hear a variation between voice and words. Polite words from an assumed bodybuilder.

"Thank you so much."

Looking at me disconnecting the phone Shrija pounced.

"Nisha, answer me - why red? Did you meet the guy?"

"Are you crazy, Shri, do you think Mr Right is such an easy person to find?"

"Nisha, if you continue at this speed I will have to look for your groom, while I am searching one for my daughter. She is thirteen already."

"Please, Shri. Stop your nonsense! You are acting like my mother. I dare you to talk to your daughter about marriage, she will think you have lost your mind. She will probably ask your hubby to admit you to a mental hospital."

"You think I don't know that Nisha? The new generation is very different. They feel the need for personal space, even before they get into their teens.

Look at me, I am forty- two and I have never had space or even a choice in most of my life's decisions. Do you see me complaining? No! You girls are too fussy."

I smile and mock back, "You are just jealous."

"Nisha, seriously, I might make fun of you sometimes, but trust me, I admire your guts to live the life of your choice," She surrenders easily.

"Thanks, Shri."

"So, Nisha what's the reason behind your happiness, if it's not your Mr. Right?"

"You know I took the day off from work yesterday, right?"

"Yes! I called but you did not pick up the phone."

"Well, I was stressed about work and this whole marriage situation. So, I took the day off and drove six hundred kilometres. It was an awesome drive."

"Who did you go with, Nisha? I know you wouldn't go alone and no girl whom we know would waste her day to go on a drive with you."

"Of course, not darling, I took my 'could-have- been' along for a drive. He was really nice."

"Really nice? Was he nice enough to become Mr. Right?" she said teasing me.

I looked at her and wondered if she is on my side or spying on me for someone else.

"No, not that way, we both have a different perspective towards life. He is genuinely nice, but not meant for me", I said, hoping that she was playing a spy and could convince my mother to let go of the Vikram situation.

"You are crazy. Don't take off again without informing me about where you are going. Not unless you want your mother to kill me. She feels that I am her replacement in office and I am supposed to take care of you as I take care of my daughter. God has gifted me with a daughter who is now thirteen years old and another who is thirteen years younger to me," Shri smiles.

"My mother has such a strong impact on everyone around me. You talk about her. Mr Bijal asks about her and her *aloo parathas*. Sometimes I feel that you guys secretly meet her in my absence. She has visited the office only four times in the last eight years. How and why are all of you so close to her? How did she manage to develop such a strong network of spies from so far?"

"I don't know what you're talking about, Nisha. I tried to call you yesterday as I heard some new issue with Kabir had cropped up."

Kabir! Again! The man is all out to ruin my life without even being present.

The drive yesterday had helped me get rid of my insecurities and helped me focus on my goal of becoming the next VP.

Now, I have to discuss him again!

I suppose I should have expected this conversation. In the corporate world, a good amount of time is spent playing games. Distract a person with mindless chatter and then subtly extract the information you need. I just wish Shri wouldn't play that game with me.

Shrija Iyer, VP Finance, age 42, my favourite person in the office.

When she does this, it makes me feel like a fool,

I guess I will play along. Let's see how far I am able to go. This is what Mr Bijal said I had to do, to become a suitable candidate for the VP position.

"What issue, Shri?" I ask, trying to sound innocent and confused.

"Don't try to pretend, Nisha. He does not say anything does mean you have the right to play your games with him."

I thought of telling her to get lost. Kabir is her friend,

not mine.

"Shri, I don't play games like Priya Madam. I don't have to. As far as Kabir is concerned, I was clear from day one. Two members of my team would assist him only for a period of two months. He was supposed to complete that project within the given time."

Yes, of course, even I know how to handle a tricky situation, I used Priya Madam's shoulder while making my point clear. There is no need for Shri to play games with me for Kabir. I love her, respect her and she should respect this simple fact.

"He did, Nisha, his project was delayed because Mr. Bijal revised the brief. Why did you withdraw those people?" she argues with me, choosing to defend her friend.

I wish she was an equally good friend to me.

"I need my complete team for upcoming jobs," I reply sternly.

"But you will be working on your projects only from the next financial year, Nisha. They are company resources and can't sit idle."

"They are not sitting idle? There is a lot of backend planning required, Shri, and you know all this much better than me. How much time you think is left for the next financial year?" I literally had to say this to prove my point.

"Those two members were his, Nisha, and he agreed to share his resources when no one was supporting you."

"Shri, I know you are Kabir's friend but that does not make me the villain."

 "Nisha, you know he has been supportive of you, whether you admit it or not".

"Shri, those two guys were absorbed by our department with an increment, which his department was not able to afford then and all of that is in consent with Mr. Bijal."

"I know you very well, Nisha. There was no need to send such a sarcastic mail, you are just an acting HOD and everyone knows who you are targeting."

I am so tired of this argument, I feel like joining my hands and pleading mercy only to make her realise that I want to shut the topic.

"I am not targeting Kabir. I learnt from him that personal life should not be mixed with professional life, I am playing my role pretty well."

"Nisha, stop acting childish. Trust me, you have reached at a very comfortable position with Bijals because of your sincerity and also by good fortune. Please don't mess things up. Maintain them. Everyone is good to you, which is a rare case out here."

"Of course, Shri, they are all good because they know Kabir would kill them if they mess with me, isn't it?"

"Now don't be that sarcastic, Nisha, I never said that. When you came here, you were just a fresher, they all have seen you blossom and love you for the simplicity that you possess. Do not take them for granted. You can be screwed any moment. This is a corporate jungle and they are all tag holders in the game."

"I am scared, Shri." I say sarcastically

After that long rant, she says, "Oh yes, don't stress about it!" And walks out.

****

I felt hurt by hearing such harsh words from my dear friend. I don't know why I even make friends at work, when it's not possible to deal with them. Here I am not even able to manage such petty issues and there I look forward to becoming VP.

Nisha dear get practical before these everyday fights hurt your chances of becoming VP.

I compose myself and wear the VP hat to resolve this issue. After considering the options, I think calling up Kabir would be the best thing to do. I haven't spoken to him in a long time and my fingers shake as I dial his extension number.

"Kab..." I clear my throat and again "Kabi...Kabir," and finally I could.

"Yes, Nisha."

His voice as always is clear, confident and magnetic— the voice that I once adored. Listening to him say my name, reminds me of the time I would call him just to hear him say - Nisha.

His voice, that once brought smile to my face, now only causes pain and disappointment.

I still have to be practical and not emotional while dealing with this issue.

"Kabir, may I know the reason you are being so nice to me?" I asked, charging at him with confidence.

Kabir, a bit surprised at this question, tries to enquire the logic behind my question.

"Meaning what, Nisha?"

"Have you given me your team members Ronak and Riyaz as a favour?"

"What sort of favour, Nisha?"

"I don't know, Kabir, as far as my understanding goes there is a clear difference between personal and professional life, for you. Personally, we are not concerned with each other and I have not taken any professional favour from you in my life."

His silence makes me feel that he is agitated, like always, and will behave in his usual self, making an attempt to shut me up.

But this time, I won't let him do that, I reassure myself.

"Yes, Nisha, you are right about that and there definitely has been no favour."

Surprisingly, he was dealing with this situation in a completely different way.

"Then what did I do wrong by taking my team members back Kabir?"

"You are right there as well, Nisha." he replied affirmatively.

"So then why is Shri making me feel like I did something wrong?"

"I don't know, Nisha, but I think you took the right decision and I am fine with it. May be you should have taken care while sending the mail. It created a misunderstanding."

I tried every trick to pick up a fight to prove him wrong, but his constant reassurance left me with no other option but to resign and put the receiver down.

I purposely wrote that nasty mail, after that argument with Mr. Bijal. I shouldn't have done that. Thankfully Kabir did not react in his usual way with it. Had it been six years back, he would have fired me for this behaviour. I used to be very scared of his temper.

He was so calm today. I think he is getting old, and that is the reason for this unusual behaviour. I feel like a fool after calling him. May be that was his intention like always, it's just that his tricks have changed, with time.

Let me try to keep Kabir out of mind and focus on work.

While wrapping up for the day, my mobile phone reminds me of the Mumbai guy I am supposed to call. Let me drop him a message to call by 9 pm.

Oh! There comes a prompt reply.

Sure, shall call you by 9. Thank you ma'am.

I find his politeness a little strange. *A sweet Mumbai guy is not normal. Maybe just like me, he isn't from Mumbai but has settled here for work. Maybe he is just faking this politeness. We will see what the truth is when he calls.*

Promptly at 9, my phone rings. Thank God I reached home.

"Hi, I am Mahesh."

"Hi, I am Nisha."

"Uh, yes. We are talking for the first time and it is a little strange. Is it as strange for you as it is for me?"

"No, Mahesh, I have been in the marriage market for years now. A seasoned player, you can say. I have been talking to guys off and on. I have become quite experienced in how to start a conversation, how to judge a conversation, what to infer from the conversation and how to end the conversation."

"Oh! Of course! The situation is quite different for me. I have just become serious about marriage. Until recently I was focusing on my career and it's now I feel that, I am settled enough in career to keep my life partner happy. I'm not saying there were no girls in my life off and on, but I was never serious."

"Why don't you become serious with them now? Were those girls not from good families or was there some other concern?"

"No, Nisha. The most unfortunate thing is that they are all married now."

"OK. So, all these girls being married have brought you to talk to me."

"I guess you can take it that way."

"So, I guess we should begin by introducing ourselves."

I smirk. I can practically see the list he is holding to conduct this conversation. Maybe this conversation will be entertaining after all.

"So, Mahesh," I tease, "how many points are there in the list that you are holding?"

"Just seven. Why?"

"Caught you," I say and start laughing.

"Nisha, I am not used to such conversations. It is quite stressful and embarrassing. If things can be made more comfortable it will be fine, else I would consider that you are not interested in talking to me."

Damn. Apparently, he cannot take a joke. I need to smooth out this conversation if I do not want to receive an angry call from my mother.

"Did I say I am not interested in talking to you, Mahesh? I was just teasing. It just sounded like you were following a script. If I wasn't interested what would you have done, called your mother to complain about me?"

"No, I will inform my sister. My mother passed away three years ago."

"Oh, I am sorry."

"Don't be."

"Mahesh, you seem like a nice guy."

"Thank you so much, it's been years since I heard a compliment from any girl."

"Really? I think you were lying earlier. I think you are shy and you have never had girls going in and out of your life."

"How do you know that?"

"Simple, no guy would sincerely admit that in the first conversation. Only a timid person trying to act cool would do that."

"I don't get it."

"Don't worry. You may start with your bullet-pointed question list now."

"There are no questions, Nisha. I would like to tell you a little about myself."

"OK, go on...." and there my assumed body-builder starts reciting a childish introduction in his heavy voice. I could sense the efforts that he must have put into preparing himself for this conversation.

"So, hi I am Mahesh, I live in Andheri East very close to my office. Originally, I am from Raipur. Professionally, I am a Marketer, working for a German MNC. I travel abroad for work often. Personally, I am a movie freak. I am always ready to go for any kind of a movie day or night. I am a bit lazy, but I love cricket—mostly watching. When I was a child, India winning matches were very important. When they lost, I would go crazy, I would not eat food for days and throw tantrums."

"You are very open about yourself." I say after he ends.

"Yes, I try to be. When I pretend to be someone else, smart girls like you catch on to the pretence."

"Is that a compliment or a complaint?" I again tease him

"What?"

"I mean is it a compliment for me—smart girls like me?"

"Indeed, Nisha."

"My, my, I am blushing."

"What else, I am the most pampered child of the house and extremely emotional."

"Are you the youngest and only male child in the family, Mahesh?"

'Yes, I have two elder sisters."

"That's why."

"Meaning?"

"Elder sisters pamper their *chotu* brothers."

"Are you an older sister?"

"Yes, and no, I have an older brother and a younger brother."

"Nice, so you know all about people it seems," he enquires

"I can read people well, probably because my mother was into psychology and I inherit her interest in the subject."

"That is nice, Nisha."

"Sometimes, yes, it works well."

"You know what I feel we could really be excellent together."

"What?"

"I mean, don't mind, I know this is not the way to propose, but you know it just slipped out. Please don't mind."

"OK."

"I think you could be my Rose."

"What?"

"I loved the movie *Titanic* when I saw it for the first time. Last scene when Jack drowns, I felt very touched, I just wanted to save him. And that very day I decided that when I would find my Rose I would not drown but would live with her happily forever. I feel you could be my Rose."

"Yeah, that sounds very filmy, Mahesh."

"Nisha, I would like to meet you to take this conversation ahead. I think I have found the love of my life in you."

"Mahesh, I understand you are a very emotional person, but you need to get control of yourself. We have barely spoken. You don't know me. I don't know you. You cannot just act as if we are meant to be together after a ten-minute conversation. I do not make serious decisions impulsively."

"That is why I am saying that we should meet, Nisha."

"Give me some time, please. I will give you a call once I make a decision. Do not call me."

"OK, Nisha,I respect your space. I shall eagerly wait for your call."

"Sure, see you. Bye."

Oh My God! This man is mad. How can anyone decide to get married to a person whom you have spoken for barely ten minutes? Men like him strengthen my decision to not fall into the marriage trap.

This is what happens when my mother just gives my phone number to random strangers.

Let me call mother, despite the late hour, hopefully I can resolve the problem quickly before it goes to a different level in the morning. I just don't trust these guys.

"Mom, that guy was insane."

"What happened with Mahesh, Nisha? Was he rude to you?"

"No, Mom, he seemed nice at first, but within ten minutes or seven and a half minutes to be precise, he claimed we were meant for each other and we should meet. You can't connect and know a person so quickly. He was just too fast."

"Nisha, please give someone a chance. He only asked to meet right? Not to get married. Do you really need to be so judgmental every time?"

"You do want me to marry only once, right?

"Nisha, don't talk nonsense. I want you to have a happy married life with the person of your choice, but it does not mean that you don't give anyone a chance."

"Mom, it's not that I don't want to give anyone a chance, but the way some of them act and speak is just so stupid. I feel like I should give them lesson on how to talk to a girl."

"Nisha, I can't talk to you any more on this. You talk to Papa."

"Mom, please, I can't just agree to marry anyone without understanding that person."

"I am done with my discussion, Nisha. Let's not talk about this topic anymore."

"OK, Mom, bye. I just wanted to let you know what happened. Sweet dreams."

Chapter 5

The next few days passed peacefully without a word from my mother. I was grateful because the pace at work had picked up. The company's Annual Conference would be taking place soon and there was a lot of work to be finished before the conference. Each team had to present their past year's achievements and goals and plans for the next year.

Typically, the technical department takes up only two projects a year to ensure quality, but this time my team in coordination with the marketing team was expected to present five innovative product concept designs with prototypes. This was the largest number of projects taken up by the company.

In addition to preparing the presentation and the designs, this year I was also responsible for presenting at the conference. Normally, being in charge would not bother me, but my conversation with Mr Bijal kept playing over in my mind and creating doubts.

I try and shrug it off, ignore my doubts and just focus on the job.

I am capable and I will prove all the doubters wrong. The first step will be to hold a meeting to discuss potential projects for the upcoming year.

I call the receptionist and admin in charge, Maria.

"Maria, please arrange a meeting with all concerned departments as soon as possible."

"Yes, Ma'am. Also, there is a bouquet for you at the reception from Mr Mahesh."

God, no! I thought cutting the conversation would serve as a message that I wasn't interested in him, but obviously it didn't work, I just hope he doesn't turn into a stalker.

I better call him up and make it clear that I am not interested.

"Hello, Mahesh."

"Hi, Nisha, I knew you would call, did you get my flowers? I just thought we could start anew with fresh flowers."

"Mahesh, I am not interested in you. I was trying to politely inform you yesterday, but I guess you do not understand subtlety. These flowers better be your first and last attempt at persuasion. If you try again, I will call the police."

He tried to convince me of his point of view, but before he could really start I said, "goodbye, Mahesh, please do not contact me again," and disconnect the phone.

Why does my mother set me up with such weird characters?

Some days, I want to meet and marry Mr Right not because I really want a life partner, but just so I can stop wasting my time on these idiots.

This nonsense is taking up precious time that I don't have any to waste.

Preoccupied with these thoughts, while walking towards the meeting hall, I wasn't paying much attention to the surrounding,

And yes I had to pay for my inattention. I encountered a 'should-have-not-happened-accident'.

I bumped into Kabir and almost fell, but he steadied me.

Embarrassed, I snarled, "I would rather fall than accept your help. Don't bother me, next time Kabir."

Walking away, I heard him say, "Did I bother her? Love this new attitude."

This incident just refreshed my conversation with Mr. Bijal and Shrija, making me hate him even more. I looked around to ensure that no one had witnessed our encounter and continued to the conference hall quietly.

I could sense Kabir watching me until I was out of sight. I hate this habit of his, since the very first day.

The six years time post break- up was not easy for me.

****

Holding a meeting in the boardroom is always a thrill. The magnificence of this room, especially the white walls, uplifts my mood. The motivational quote frames charge my mind.

I was a part of the designing team when Mr. Bijal gave the brief to renovate it, a few years ago.

This meeting is an opportunity to learn and educate. It is a chance to feel normal, without the additional drama and pressure of the dangling VP position.

"Good evening, everyone, thank you for coming."

"Good evening, Nisha. I see, you are getting an early start for the annual conference, as usual." says Ryan, the Marketing Head.

"Sir, with your permission I would like to begin the discussion"

"Please go ahead."

"Sir, for next year we have a few product developments in the pipeline. For two of the projects, I will require marketing and sales inputs."

"OK. What do you have in your mind?"

"During our last discussion, we identified scope within the residential buildings. Societies are facing space issues concerning basement-parking areas. However, we did not discuss the problem in detail."

"Yes, I remember. We need to do consumer research to understand how to solve this problem."

"Exactly, Sir. I would like us to conduct this research as soon as possible to develop a solution to this problem. A solution will not only enable us to cater to new projects, but also existing projects."

"Noted. I suggest that you send your technical team along with the marketing people for on-site visit and get a first-hand understanding."

"Good idea, Sir, I shall do that in the next two days. This will help us get some idea and post the meeting we can start with the consumer survey."

"Yes. Ganesh, please help the technical team with permissions and ask the sales team to send their people along," Ryan instructs one of his managers.

"Thank you Sir" says Nisha

"Is there anything else that you need from me, Nisha?" asks Mr Ryan. He is a known name in the field of marketing. He headed the marketing team for one of the most renowned real estate companies before Mr. Bijal managed to lure him to the Bijal Group with a salary offer that was five times more than his then package."

"No, Sir, this is all we require right now." I reply.

The meeting concludes at around 10:30 pm.

I feel grateful that even if the senior management has doubts about my abilities, my team and the departments I coordinate with, have trust in me. The meeting was long, but everyone took it seriously. The departments worked together like a collective brain to resolve all problems—small and big.

Thank God, Kabir did not turn up, else it would have been a mess. I was scared that he would enter during the meeting and the meeting would be a disaster. Most people in the company enjoy his absence from group meetings.

And after that embarrassing moment, I would not have been able to handle his presence today.

****

As I headed to my car, I checked my phone and the sight of sixty-five missed calls gave me a shock. Most of them were from Mother.

With a thumping heart and trembling fingers, I called home, Mom never calls me these crazy number of times.

Thankfully, there was nothing serious; she was just curious about my plans for the end of the month.

After reprimanding mom for scaring me, I answer her question.

"Mom, I have my Annual Conference in Goa at the end of the month, I will not be in town. Why, what happened?"

"Nothing Papa has to come to visit a doctor in Mumbai, he wanted to check if you are there?

"Is anything serious Mom?"

"No, Nisha."

"Mom, are you sure it's not serious? Should I try and get someone to replace me at the conference?"

"Don't worry, Nishu. Papa is just coming for a routine check-up."

"OK, Mom."

"Is everyone in the company going along with you?"

"No, only manager level and above, but Bijal Sir is coming only for the award ceremony."

"OK, take care."

"Bye, Mom."

Papa is so careless about his health. He should stop working and start enjoying life. I don't know why he doesn't understand. At times, I really feel like asking Papa and Mom to come and stay with me. I can rent a house in Prabha-Devi, next to Siddhivinayak temple so that they can visit the temple whenever they wish. Hinduja Hospital is also nearby so we can deal with any health issue easily.

****

Nagpur

Nisha's mother is stressed and upset. At 53, she looks really young. She, like Nisha, is not very tall and not very fair, yet she is graceful and elegant. Sitting on her light brown sofa, in her light brown sari, she couldn't help but worry about all her children, especially Nisha.

Just as she is about to head to bed her elder son, Suraj, arrives.

"Suraj, is this the time to come home?"

''Mom relax—I am not a kid, I was travelling for work, I was in Gwalior and I told you before leaving."

"I am sorry, it slipped from my mind."

Seeing his mother a bit lost he enquires, "Mom, you are getting worked up for no reason. What is going wrong with you?"

"Suraj, I am really worried about Nisha."

"Why, Mom, she is doing so well. We are all so proud of her."

"I am not, Suraj."

"Mom, come on. She is the only girl from our family to have such a successful career and at this young age."

"She is a girl, Suraj, and that is why I am more worried. She will be thirty soon and still nowhere close to getting married. I don't know how to get her to settle down."

"Mom, she will find her life partner, trust her."

"Trust her, right! You obviously don't remember how she tricked us and ran away to Mumbai."

"Mom, I remember, but I still trust her."

"And that is why she keeps taking advantage of you."

"What do you mean, Mom?"

"Suraj, I know you love your sister but she doesn't have to live like a man. She will turn thirty in a couple of months and if she doesn't get married soon, there will be no one there to marry her. At thirty-two, you still have time to get married, she doesn't. How can I not despair when I can see where my daughter's life is heading?"

"Mom, you are overreacting."

"Listen, Suraj, you are lost in your life and can't see what your parents can. She has been lying to us since her schooldays only to get what she wants."

"I think you should relax, Mom, I will talk to her."

It was a difficult time for Chandra family. Three children — two boys and one daughter — of marriageable age — two of them above 28. Both the sons doing well in

business, the daughter at a good position in corporate world—yet none of them were serious about tying the knot. In a small town like Nagpur, the family had become a topic of discussion amongst neighbours and relatives.

Dhara Chandra, known for her frank and candid remarks, had almost stopped attending social functions. Her popularity as a mother to three successful children had declined due to rumours and gossip about their unmarried status. She was aware that the taunts were mostly because they were jealous, but she could not escape from the reality that something was seriously missing in her family.

It was difficult for her to face this social ostracisation but she couldn't find the courage to share these details with her children.

Meanwhile, Nisha, unaware of the developments at home, was busy building her career.

****

Mumbai

Time passed very swiftly and before I could realise, it was time to go to the conference.

Everyone gather at the office to head to Goa. All members including the senior staff are travelling by bus. Just like every year they will play *Anstakshari*, laugh at jokes and reveal their humorous side to the subordinates, who would pretend as if they have seen their hidden talent for the first time in this trip.

Mars Land, one of the best properties in Goa is the chosen destination for this conference. It is a huge property with lots of space and greenery around, unlike Mumbai, where we see only moving vehicles and running people. Many say that Mumbai is a place to earn money and Goa is to spend. Unfortunately, knowing this does not free you from Mumbai's smog to enjoy the fresh air of Goa on a regular basis.

For many of staff, this was their first visit to Goa and they were thrilled to be there.

The first day was simple and relaxing. We spent our time sightseeing, on the lovely beaches, enjoying breeze and the sun. Members of the group who had visited Goa previously complained about missing the Goa Carnival. Some thought that the conference should have been two weeks earlier so that they could attend the carnival as well. Others thought the delay in date was because the company wanted to save on expenses. Many were unaware of the enormity of the festival.

In the midst of all this, I made a constant effort to remain around my set of close friends, just like last three years. I normally interact with everyone in the office, but during events like these, I exert more care to ensure that I could avoid certain presences.

The next two days were spent indoors listening to department presentations.

Unlike other company directors, Mr Bijal did not have imaginary long teeth to suck blood, or horns to hit the employees. He has well-defined company policies to keep everyone in place. So there weren't many reasons for people to talk about him behind his back.

My presentation was appreciated for its fresh perspective, yet I did not win. Someone else stole the show, the same someone that I was trying to avoid. The same someone who wanted to come with me to Goa after we got married. The same one whom I hate so much.

Every achievement he makes, drives me to set myself a new challenge, and next year for sure I will win the presentation award.

Today is the last day and the day the promotions will be announced. I don't know what will happen, and remembering my conversation with Mr. Bijal has left my confidence shaky.

In nervousness, I brushed my boring black straight hair for over an hour, until they were at the verge of breaking. I tried a little bit of kajal to my famous- fish-cut eyes, my best feature, as they make me look like a Bengali girl and got me, my childhood nickname 'girl with magic eyes'. I feel that adding heels to my outfit not only gives me that little height, but also boosts my confidence. I am very well aware that I am the shortest woman at the conference.

Hopefully by presenting myself well, no one sees my nerves. I still curse the day, when I got into the argument with Mr Bijal. I really want the promotion to VP of Technical. If the position goes to someone else I will resign from the company.

I have given this company eight long years and so much profit. If Kabir or anyone from his team becomes the VP of my department, he will change the entire structure. I am the one who has made this team successful.

Wish I were a jugadu like Priya Madam. She does all her settings well before the game starts. She is like the participants on Big Boss. She pretends well, plays well, uses well and discards well. At the end, she manages to achieve all of this without offending anyone. If she were an actual participant on Big Boss, she would be the winner.

I don't play well. I am definitely not tactful when I should be. This is why she is where she is and I keep crying about my hard work. This is 'why' the management has doubts about my abilities and me.

I give myself a pep talk trying to calm down.

Calm down Nisha. You are overreacting because you lost the best presentation award. Don't worry, you have it in you. You have come much further than most people in such a short time. Whether you get the position or not, you are a challenger and should be proud of that. Yes, the corporate world is like a Big Boss game, either you win or you learn to play it your way.

All the dread, the worry, was for nothing. The evening finally makes me VP of the Technical Department of the company. Many are happy for me yet some are not, but that is part and parcel of the game.

The minute the event was over, I call Mother.

"Mom, I made Vice President of the Technical Department."

"Are you mad, Nisha?"

"What? Mom, did you hear what I said? I made VP."

"I know what you said, Nisha. Do you even understand how difficult you are making life for us?"

"How does my receiving a promotion make life difficult for you, Mom?"

"The more your pay package increases, the more difficult it gets for us to find prospects for your marriage. You need to leave your job and come back home."

"Mom, are you crazy? Do you really understand what you are saying?"

"Yes, I understand that I should have not allowed you to work. You never gave us that option, Nisha. Before we could plan a lovely life for our daughter, you played with our emotions and ran away."

"Mom, please, can't you just be happy and proud of me. Whatever I did is in the past, trust me that was the right decision. Just see how far have I come, you guys decided to marry me off before I could even complete my education, I just chose not to. Everyone is proud of me, except you. And I did not run away, I had a job. It is so difficult to talk to you sometimes."

"Don't talk to me, if you have such news to share. It makes no difference to me. If you want money, tell me, we have enough properties, you don't have to work."

"Mom, I have to go. Bye. I think I woke you up from sleep. No mother on this earth would react like this to her child's achievements. I wish I was your son."

"You are not, and don't try to be one."

I disconnected the phone, I never thought mom would not be proud of my achievements. *Maybe she just doesn't understand. Mom has never seen life from a career perspective. A daughter with a career, responsibilities outside the home and rising up the career path is strange for her. Papa manages the financial aspects of her life, from buying our homes to paying the electricity bill. It didn't help, all her children were more like Papa—independent and driven. Maybe that is why there is a gap between what she expects and what I expect. She wants me to be understanding and I want her to be understanding.*

I choose a dark corner to celebrate my success with Ms. Nisha Chandra (myself), when the entire office is enjoying the party. Instead of being happy, I am upset because Nisha Chandra's (my) mother is upset with my promotion. As always, I was lost in my own world, and did not notice, that I was being watched.

He saw me leaving the room and followed me, hoping to get a chance to talk - but I would not allow him to affect me anymore.

Thank god, I saw him at the right time, he steps forward towards me from the other corner of the room and I step back ensuring that he is able to see the annoyance, avoidance and rejection in my eyes. Thankfully, he gets the message and does not move ahead.

He stood there, as I slowly and deliberately moved away. Keeping a firm grip on my emotions, I head to the lift and then to my room. I didn't want to draw any attention and leave for Mumbai peacefully in the morning.

****

Back to Mumbai

I wonder how to handle this situation with Mother.

Should I apply Shreyas' technique to manage her?

Shreyas, my Chotu brother adds enthusiasm to my adventurous side and serves as my lifeline during troubled times. He is extremely different from Suraj bhai and even myself.

Shreyas is the popular one, especially with ladies. He showers them with attention making them feel important. He does it to me as well. We go shopping together; he gives me honest opinions on my selections and pampers me like crazy. He is the only person in my family to whom I never have to lie and I can be myself with. What I love most about him is the way he manages Mom.

When we were younger, he had a close friend, Shalini whose mom made excellent samosas, which he brought home. When Mom saw the box of samosas, she started questioning us. Mom did not like us having friends of the opposite gender.

Shreyas smoothly diverted the questioning and stayed out of trouble by quickly distributing the samosas and telling Mom that my best friend, Preeti, had made them. Everyone enjoyed samosas including Mom, who is an excellent cook. The revelation that Preeti could cook is probably what had made my Mom so happy and in the excitement she did not bother to ask any more questions. I had to ask Preeti to actually lie if Mom ever asked her and the poor girl chose to learn how to make good samosas, as she was not good at lying.

He used a similar ruse when he was caught having dinner with a girl. He pretended not to notice Mom and Papa at the restaurant while making sure Mom could see her clearly. He then proceeded to avoid Mom for the next few days. Mom called me in fury to find out what I knew about the situation. Luckily, I could honestly say nothing. Shreyas confused mom by bringing a different girl home. He let Mom meet her and speak to her.

Mom, completely confused and agitated, called me to get answers. She wanted to know what Shreyas was up to and if he was seeing a girl and if yes then which girl. I tried my best to calm her down, but I was not very successful.

The minute she put down the phone, I remember messaging Shreyas to understand what had transpired.

"What is this girl issue, dude? What are you doing to Mom?"

"Relax, Di, don't get worked up."

"But what happened?"

"Nothing yaar, Kavita and I are not sure of where our relationship will head. I still need time to settle in a career and Mom gets so hyper over everything. I can't even introduce normal friends to her."

"Who did you take home today?"

"Shraddha."

"Why?"

"I want to confuse Mom. The more girls she meets, the more confused she will get and hopefully she will stop pestering me about the 'girls in my life'."

"You are mad. Don't get into trouble."

"Don't worry, Di, let me get back to work now."

"Bye."

It was a funny incident, given the way my mother is, Shreyas managed to send across his message to her in the most intelligent and polite way possible. Yes, there was a mental tiff, but it was worth it. Sometimes, I really feel Shreyas is a good fit for the corporate world. After that day, Mom stopped interfering in his life.

Suraj is steady as a rock. He has been in a committed relationship with his girlfriend Roma for years, but his relationship is still awaiting parental approval. I have never been able to commit to anyone, long term.

Maybe I can employ a similar tactic as Shreyas to convince Mom that I can be trusted to manage my marriage situation on my own.

****

Chapter 6

Nagpur

Nisha's mom had one basic fear—if Suraj got approval to marry Roma, a girl outside their caste, then Nisha's marriage prospects would worsen.

Neither Dhara nor her husband were rigid and that was one of the reasons they had always encouraged their children to excel. Unfortunately, the community they belonged to was very narrow-minded, despite the new generation working and studying abroad. If Nisha had someone in mind for marriage then things would have been different. In their community, girls typically get married in their late teens or early twenties, but Nisha was almost 30. They could neither announce their interest in looking for prospects outside their caste nor was Nisha agreeing to marry any guy within their community.

Until Nisha got married, Dhara couldn't even think of Roma and Suraj.

Mr Chandra was equally worried about the whole situation.

****

Mumbai

Who would call me early in the morning?

Suraj Bhai, but he never calls this early.

"Bhai, what happened? Why are you calling so early?"

"Nisha, Dad had a heart attack in middle of the night."

My mind froze. All I could think of was that I had to go home now. Papa, don't die. I am coming home, please be there when I get home. Papa, please get well soon.

I don't remember the rest of the conversation. I only remember that the minute I got off the phone, I quickly booked tickets to Nagpur.

I have to go home now. I need to see my Father. I cannot imagine my life without him.

Papa, how many times have I told you to take care of yourself, to sleep on time and to eat on time.

I have even asked you to stop working, because you are growing older and you shouldn't be under so much pressure. But, no, you refuse to listen. All you do is repeat the same words to me. You just don't understand that there is a thirty-year age gap between us. I am young and can deal with the stress of my lifestyle while you are not thirty anymore, it is time for you to enjoy a more relaxing lifestyle.

You still insist on working despite having three capable children who can support you in every way. Sometimes I feel you forget that we live in a modern India, where head of the family is no longer the sole bread winner. We are all capable of earning.

Please be well, Papa. Please.

As I boarded the plane, I realised that I hadn't informed anyone at work that I won't be in, I quickly send a message to HR and my superior to let them know of my sudden travel plan. Thankfully, they sanctioned my leave at once. They offered to help and asked if I need anything. The best part of working at the Bijal Group is the fact that it is run by genuine people who know how to value their employees.

****

Nagpur

As I reach home, the atmosphere scares me—my ever-chattering mother is silent, my ever-playful younger brother looks intense and mature, my elder brother who is constantly travelling for work is at home with his girlfriend, who is managing the house like she is already a part of the family.

It is terrifying. Did Papa suffer another heart attack while I was travelling? Did his condition worsen?

Before I could draw any conclusion or ask any question, my brother gave me a reassuring smile.

"The doctors said it was a minor attack he will be all right. Be quiet, he is resting in his room."

I said to myself, *Thank God*, before asking him what else the doctor had to say.

"The doctor said we need to make sure he is comfortable. No crying in front of him. Act natural. Don't do anything to increase his stress levels."

I nod. I can see the determination on their faces to keep Papa, the head of our family, happy. We will do everything to ensure he has a long life.

****

I cannot help but observe the strange atmosphere within my home. I almost feel like a visitor—a stranger in my own home. I decide to talk to my mother, hoping to find a way to ease the tension and contribute towards my father's recovery and happiness.

"Mom, how are you doing? You have not spoken to me since I have come. We have not even had our usual argument on meeting each other."

"Nishu, I don't want to argue with anyone. All of you are free to live your life how you want. I only know that your father is my life and I want to live the rest of my life with him, not without him."

"Mom, please don't say such things."

"I mean it, Nishu. For his health and happiness, I will do anything."

"Even accept Roma despite your hatred for her Mother?"

"Nisha, I never hated her mother. Roma is my son's choice. I have realised that life is precious. Suraj and Roma love each other. If I want the love of my life to be with me, why shouldn't they have the same option?"

"I love you, Mom!"

"I love you too. Now go rest."

"Nisha," she stopped me, "When are you going back to work? You have been given some important responsibility I believe."

"Nothing is more important than all of you. I am not going anywhere right now."

"Do you have enough leaves?"

"Yes, Mom, I have sufficient leave. I have not utilised most of my leaves in the past eight years; I can stay here for months without a problem. Mom, how did this stroke happen?"

She looks at me wearily and answers, "We were arguing about your marriage. You are almost thirty years old but not married yet. We want you to have someone special in your life, but I guess for you, your promotion to VP is more important. I wanted him to talk to you about settling down sooner, but he said that I should let you be and he will find you a husband of your calibre. He feels you are a very sensible and capable person, and it is not easy to get to the level you have reached. He is very proud of you and wants you to pursue your career.

While we were arguing, he suddenly could not breathe and started complaining of chest pain. Luckily, Suraj was at home and so things went smoothly. We rushed him to the hospital where the doctor diagnosed him with a minor attack. Roma came with just one call. She took charge of everything. I have accepted Roma and now I accept whatever decision you make about your life."

"Mom," I began, "I didn't mean to..."

She cut me off. Don't stress yourself. Just go to your room and rest. Roma cleaned up. She will be sharing the room with you for some days.

"Maa," I pleaded.

"Go, Nisha, let me go and be with Papa. I want to give him all my time now."

I was in tears. My mother loves my father so much. She just cannot live without him. God, please don't let anything wrong happen to Papa. They are so happy together. I do not want to be the cause of their unhappiness and ill health.

****

Nisha was unaware of the actual situation at home and had her own notions about it.

Roma is my elder brother's girlfriend. They met and fell in love in college. They remained together through her move to Jabalpur Science College and back. Today, she is a doctor and he is a settled businessman. The only reason they are not married is the problems between our mothers. *One is behaving like Lalita Pawar and the other like Shashi Kala, from list of bollywood movie moms.* It's ironic, Roma and Bhai are struggling to get married; their mothers are standing in their way. While I am struggling to not be pushed around the marriage pyre with any random stranger; my mother is pushing me for marriage.

However, once Papa is better, I am sure things will change. Mom is no longer opposed to Roma. Soon, Mom will get at least one wedding that she has been dreaming about.

I sometimes wonder if getting married is really worth, and then I look at Mom's love for Papa and even Roma's love for Suraj. Yes their dedication does get me to think that there is something positive about this institution.

If career, passion and independence were so important then the world would have been full of career-oriented, competitive and successful professionals, but that breed is still comparatively small. We as a race, value relationships and love. Maybe Mr Right is just a perception, someone needs to be given a chance to be Mr Right.

How would anyone know what is right for me, until I let him know?

****

Suraj was sitting with Roma in the balcony, discussing about the difficult time Chandras were going through.

"Roma, I am sorry for making things so difficult for you. Thank you for being with me at every step."

"Suraj, please. There is no reason to thank me. You are my family and they are yours. I'm happy to do whatever I can."

"No, Roma, it's been years, but I still haven't been able bring you into my home formally. I can understand your mother's concern. You have still given me those years of your life."

"My life is with you, Suraj, and trust me, everything will be fine."

"I hope so. Mom is not bad at heart, but whatever she said to your mother was only because she is worried about Nisha's marriage."

"I understand, Suraj, you don't have to explain anything."

****

Dhara sees them from the balcony of her room.

They look so nice together, a young and energetic couple, so much in love that they don't mind sacrificing their life for my daughter. I know Roma is the best daughter-in-law we could have. It's so cruel on my part to take away her happiness in the struggle to find happiness for my own daughter. I can't do that anymore.

Since the first time Roma came to the Chandra house, I deliberately created barriers, making it difficult for Suraj to even discuss this topic. On the other hand, I never floated his matrimonial proposal to anyone within the community. From day one, I was clear that Roma would be my daughter-in-law, but making it public with an unmarried, almost same age daughter would have been a bad idea. So I played a psychological game to favour everyone. Being a psychology student, I learnt this art of mind management in college. Roma being a psychiatrist herself understood me and out of respect silently followed the game without any questions.

No, I can't do injustice to my children because of the fear of society. Whether my daughter finds a groom within the society or not, I can't let Roma and Suraj suffer because of my fears.

She goes to them.

Suraj was holding Roma's hand, as they were engrossed in their conversation. Dhara makes them aware of her presence. They immediately leave each other's hands and stand straight, little conscious.

"Roma, I am sorry, *beta*, for hurting your feelings."

"No, please don't say that Maa. I respect you and I am happy with any decision you take."

"I know, *beta*, if I don't give you my consent then both of you will not get married."

"We love and respect you, Mom, and you know that very well. Family first," says Suraj.

Dhara looks at Roma with tears in her eyes, choked with emotions, she struggles to speak.

Roma holds her hand and reassures Dhara with her eyes, conveying her feelings. Dhara finally completes her sentence, "Please tell your mother that I am coming to meet her and bring my daughter-in-law home forever."

Suraj looks at their face glittering with smiles, takes them both around in his arms, and kisses his mother on her head. He is determined to get happiness for his family. Being the eldest son does not only mean taking up the financial responsibility, it means a lot more. "Mom, I promise you, I will bring back your smile."

"I am happy now, son. My happiness is in all of your happiness."

"Mom, Nisha will be married soon and that is my promise. I know that I have been blinded by my love for her. I forgot that she is a girl and has to start her family life. If she is lost and unable to make a decision, it does not mean that I should let her continue on this disillusioned journey. As an elder brother, it's my duty to guide her in this phase."

They smile looking at each other. The elder son is now going to play his role. The daughter-in-law will soon come home. The daughter of the family will get her Mr Right.

****

I was tired of waiting for Roma, so, I go down to find her. Oh there she is, about to sit down at the dinner table with mother. I am so happy to see both of them together.

"Roma"

"Shh, Nisha, Papa is sleeping, don't be loud."

Now this is what I call - family connection.

"You will be staying in my room, Roma." – I whisper, loud enough for her to listen.

"Hope you don't mind, Nisha." – She whispers back.

"Not at all, actually I was waiting for you. Bhai told me that you sleep early." – I say going close to her.

"Yes, I do as I have to wake up early in the morning to manage the house and get to work."

"OK, will you be able to manage?"

"Nisha, I don't have a hectic lifestyle like yours. Suraj

keeps telling me about how hard you work. We are all very proud of you."

"Oh please, Roma."

"Come on, come have dinner with us." She insists as I sit next to her.

"Yes," I felt like a guest of honour in my own family.

Bonding time for the women of the house is very touching. It feels like we are in a scene of a Bollywood film story, *Hum Saath Saath Hain*, but thankfully without tears and background music.

In real life, the drama is twenty times less than it is exaggerated in films and television, but yes, drama does exist. Without drama life would become very superficial. Everyday dramas add some flavour of life.

Without singing an emotional family song we had a peaceful dinner, we cleaned the kitchen and went to our respective rooms.

****

"Nisha, life must be very hectic there in Mumbai. How do you manage?"

"You get used to it after sometime Roma. Bhai visits me once in two or three months, and we even shop for you."

"Yes, and I love your choices, your taste is very classy."

"Did you wear the makeup Bhai got last time?"

"The makeup kit is too expensive. I am going to save it and use it for the special occasion."

"What special occasion? Life is too short, Bhabhi dear. Looks like Maa has finally given you the green signal. It is time for you to come home permanently. Next time I come home, I want it to be for your wedding."

"First, we will get you married, Nisha. Only then will we plan our wedding. In fact, your D-Day is the special occasion for which I am saving the make-up. It better be soon."

"Roma, I don't know when I will get married, but trust me if I keep meeting guys or talking to them with the speed my Mother makes me to talk to them, I will not end-up getting married. It feels like a desperate effort to get rid of me."

"Don't think of it that way, we will find you the guy of your choice."

"Please, Roma, there is no guy of choice."

"So then, what do you plan to do?"

"Roma, I want to do something for my parents' happiness."

"Like what?"

"Before I tell you my plan, you need to accept that I am mad and very confused when it comes to making a choice for a lifelong partner."

"OK, accepted. Now what, Nisha?"

"Now you tell me, what would you do if you were me and as uncertain about choosing the wrong person."

"Oh, Madam, have you been waiting all evening to trap me in your room to discuss this?"

"Please Roma, don't be angry. It's just that you are a doctor that deals with the mind. I was just hoping you would give me advice like you would to a patient."

"What?"

"Please, please, tell me what will you do?"

"My situation is very different, Nisha. I fell in love with your brother and decided to spend the rest of my life with him. I don't want anyone or anything else."

"Roma, your situation may be ideal, but my life is not as simple. I am not normal and I definitely can't seem to pick a life partner. Vikram was a gentleman, but I couldn't even agree to marry him."

"Oh OK. In that case, I would place my trust in the people who are very close to me and say 'yes' to their decision without hesitation."

"You mean blindly?"

"Nisha, you asked me and I told you genuinely, what I would have done if I could not trust myself."

"Really?"

"Yes, Nisha, you have to believe in life. Look at Mom and Papa, look at Suraj and me, we are all together because there is a belief, not just in ourselves but also in each other and in the people around us. I knew Mom would change her views about me and she did, right?"

"Right."

"Now sleep. All will be well. I have to wake up early;

there is a lot of work to be done before Papa goes to the hospital for his check-up."

"Goodnight."

****

Instead of going to the hospital with papa, I decide to stay at home and consider what I can do to contribute to Papa's health and happiness.

I enter our family pooja room, a big room with hundreds of Gods and Goddess pictures neatly placed. It is the cleanest room of our house. We fear God for our Karma. Each picture has proper tika placed at the centre of the face. Each Hindu God has a reason behind its existence. All of them are in-charge of one code-of-conduct that we as human are supposed to follow.

I have forgotten names of few, which shows how much I have disconnected from my roots in the past few years. But their pictures remind me of the stories dadi narrated when I was a child.

I pray to each one of you for my father's health and my family's happiness. Please give me wisdom to decide my role in the happiness of our family. I don't want to take them for granted anymore nor do I want to be the cause of arguments between Mom and Papa. I am sorry for not visiting you all these years.

Roma's solution to my problem is worth considering.

May be I should accept it as a viable option. If not a permanent solution, at least a temporary one until Papa recovers.

I can pull off such dramas with ease in any case.

"What does the report say, Bhai?" I ask as they step in.

"Papa is out of danger now. All we need to do is keep him happy and stress-free."

"Thank God! I am so happy, Bhai."

"Even we are relaxed, Nisha, now our only focus is to keep him happy."

These words from Bhai are so relaxing, I wanted to say, 'Bhai, I will get married', but it's difficult, so, I leave the room and go to see papa.

I am so happy to see him out of danger.

"Papa, I love you. Please don't take stress because of me. I will do whatever you say."

Papa looks delighted with my words; he puts his hand over my head to bless me with a smiling face. All his children are independent and he never forced us into anything we were not convinced of. He believes that we are mature enough to decide right and wrong and this is why I love him so much.

Shreyas had been observing Nisha's moves from the time she came out to receive them. He could sense that the environment at home was affecting his sister. For the past several years, she had been away from home, disconnected from the family and has become very independent, unable to mould her decisions as per the feelings of the rest of them. Mentally she had drifted a lot, despite of being emotionally bonded to the family. He tries to cheer her up.

"Di, come let's go out for coffee. It's been long since we went out for a date," he says, winking at Roma.

Roma gets the message and pipes in. "Am I not invited, Shreyas?"

"Bhabhi, we will go on a special date, I need to convince Bhai as we can't take him along."

"Oh really? There must be some special agenda for our date then?"

"Of course, Bhabhi, you can decide the agenda."

"OK, my dear, then I hope the girl is final, so I can give you an approval and convince Maa."

"Oh God, Bhabhi are you also aware about my pranks."

"You are the most popular bachelor in town, my dear."

"Is that so? That is amazing! Di, are you going to get ready, or should I carry you out in the pyjamas you are wearing?"

"Don't you dare do that, Shreyas, last time you picked me up, you dropped me. I will kill you if you try that again."

"Aww, my dear sister, please get ready then, I am waiting for you in the car. I can't take you like this, it's a question of my reputation."

"Please, Shreyas, I am not in a mood right now."

"Di, we are going and that's final."

Seeing us indulge in a conversation that was headed

nowhere, Suraj pushes me to get ready for the outing and I force myself to go.

**

For Suraj it was very important to find the right guy for his sister. He wanted to take charge of that responsibility and ease his parents' worries. Nothing was as difficult, his sister was an ambitious, career woman but not ruthless. She had spent the past few years tackling corporate power and arrogance, but was not insensitive. It's just that she was not able make a decision about marriage and he wanted to help her with that.

Nisha was finally relaxed. The undercurrent of tension at home wasn't easy to deal with.

Yes, I feel nice as I sip my favourite coffee, but it isn't easy to smile when your dear ones are upset. Do I need to go back to Mumbai? Can't I make my life here with my near and dear ones? Can't I start my own construction equipment design firm? My brothers are excellent at business and I am good in my stream, why should I fight a battle in someone else's land, where I have to keep proving my worth over and over, when I can start my own company?

I don't know if it's the right decision but before I make up my mind or take Shreyas and Suraj Bhai into confidence, I should carefully plan and develop a solid strategy.

My career is important for me and so is my family. I don't want to take any decision in haste. I want to explore all the possible options that would bring me peace of mind and happiness to the family.

Suddenly I am brought back to reality by Shreyas with a rocking idea.

"Di, you know what, we should all shift to Mumbai."

"What? Why do you think so?"

"It's a better place to live and there is so much you can do out there. Nagpur is still a small town."

"You are right Shreyas. That's a great idea." If I move to Nagpur, it would still be a compromise but if my family shifts to Mumbai, then it would be an upgrade.

"Di I have some friends there who are planning to start their own project and I want to join them."

"Should I start hunting for a place then? We can all stay together."

"Relax, Di, there is still time. For Bhai and me it would be a great shift, but Mom and Papa might not be able to survive there, away from our dear relatives. We must wait for some time."

"Hmmm..."

I am happy with this thought. Once we are together, there will be less hassle. They will finally understand the difficulties of my life. Sitting in a slow moving city like Nagpur and judging my life in Mumbai is not fair in any case.

All of this would require a lot of planning. A few more dramas, coupled with some made-up stories with a topping of some make-belief lies would have to be fabricated. It's so difficult to get the Chandras on track otherwise.

As Nisha thinks about her next move to bring stability in her life, she doesn't realise that she her thoughts were becoming selfish again.

Principally her views are different from her family's beliefs. They feel she needs support to settle her personal life, while she felt that they need to be coaxed away from the pressures and obligations of society. There was a difference in perspective from both the sides.

Back home Suraj and Roma were also working on their strategy.

Chapter 7

It was evening time and all the siblings were sitting together. Roma was coming in and out of the kitchen where she was helping Dhara.

It seems like a good opportunity to broach the topic while everyone was around.

"Suraj Bhai, I feel we should shift to Mumbai."

I could see Shreyas getting the shock of his life with my statement. He seem to have thought I would not take his words seriously. More than being shocked he was worried, if Suraj found out that this idea was his brainchild he would get a hard punch from elder brother. As it is both brothers were not on the same page when it came to work. They have their own style of working.

Their business is the same but their style of operating is different. Their client base and vendors are also different. Some like Suraj's way of working, as it seems more mature, long-term, trustworthy, traditional and consistent, while other's like to work with Shreyas. Shreyas works on attractive rate deals with an aggressive on-the-spot bulk sale strategy. His rates could not be compared to even the manufacturer's rates. It was impossible to understand how he made his package deals, but neither was he operating at a loss nor was there any unfair trade practice. They both had expanded their business in opposite directions, not intruding in each other's territory, yet supporting each other whenever required.

I wouldn't get Shreyas into trouble for sure but definitely want bhai to share his views.

"What do you mean, Nisha?"

"Bhai, I feel Papa needs really good care and Mumbai has good health facilities, far better than what we have here."

"And what makes you say that?" He starts bombarding.

"Bhai, this is not a place to live, everyone is interested in everyone's life. People gossip for no reason and I feel at this age Mom and Papa should get some peace."

"Really do you feel so?" he gets sarcastic and I start losing my ground.

"Yes, Bhai, I do. Moreover, I will now be given accommodation by company, a big house for us."

"Nisha, they would be at peace if you agree to settle down. Nothing more can be more peaceful for them."

"Bhai, the moment I get the good guy I will settle down, and that is a promise."

"You have too high expectations Nisha. You are being so unrealistic; at times I feel that you are confused about what you want in life."

"I am not, Bhai."

"You are, Nisha, I want you to accept the reality of life. I feel you are too insecure about the future and that is why you do not accept that the fact that - life is to share with others, we are born to share and care. You have to get out of this shell that you have placed yourself in."

"Bhai, I am in not any shell, I don't understand what you are trying to say?"

I can never understand why people just don't let things be. It's my life and I am very protective about this subject. I hate it when anyone else other than Mom, opens up this discussion. I am so used to her constant nagging now that her words have stopped bothering me. Bhai is trying to convince me about something that I am already convinced. We are just talking in circles, he should make his point before I leave the discussion mid-way and go to my room.

"Do you trust me, Nisha?"

"Of course, Bhai, do I need to prove?"

"No, you don't, all you need to do is listen to me."

"OK, I am listening, Bhai," as if I have any other option. It seems like I have opened up a wrong subject at a wrong time.

"Nisha, Papa needs to be kept happy. What if he does not feel comfortable there?"

"Bhai, we can always come back."

"Moving cities is such a big decision and you want me to uproot them twice if they don't feel comfortable? Don't you think that is too much for your parents to take at this age?"

"Why?"

"You know how people are. They will say that the Chandras gave up. They could not take a little criticism so they ran off and started staying with their unmarried daughter. God knows what she was doing alone in Mumbai all these years. Have you considered how much worse the situation will be if they then decide to come back, with you still being unmarried?"

"Bhai, I seriously feel you are overreacting? They can always announce a short term visit to their daughter's place."

"Really? Do you think papa will stay in your house for that long a time?"

"Yes, if we convince him, he will. I don't see it that difficult. Nobody knows about the future, Bhai. It might turn out to be the best and most successful deals ever made by the Chandras."

"So my little sis is behaving like a business woman"

"Bhai, I am being practical. You never know about the future. Whatever calculated risks you take, how much ever good relations you have, what has to happen will happen. Your game is already decided, all you need to do is play it well."

"Wow, I am impressed. Ok I propose a deal to you, my headstrong, super successful, extra smart, ambitious sister."

"What deal, Bhai?"

"You get married to a guy of my choice and I promise Maa and Papa will come and stay with you in Mumbai. I will make this impossible, possible for you, if you agree to me."

"What, Bhai, have you gone mad? What is impossible in taking Mom and Papa to Mumbai?" I could clearly sense that Bhai was deliberately trapping me into this conversation.

"Their current mind and health status makes it impossible for you to take them along. And what is wrong in my proposal? If you agree to it then I convince them."

"Bhai, have you even asked them if they are not convinced? And you are making a deal out of my life."

"And what about their life? Is that not worth considering?

"Bhai, my family is the most important to me and I am only proposing the best option." I found myself failing to give the exact answers. I was not talking my mind, rather dancing to his tunes.

"So you think we will propose the worst?"

"Bhai, I didn't say that." He was engaging me into a different level of conversation altogether.

"Then why do you expect us to agree when you don't display an iota of trust in us? Have I ever let you down?"

"No, Bhai."

"Don't you trust your brother?"

"I have faith in you, Bhai, I trust you more than myself."

"Then why are you so apprehensive about agreeing my proposal? If the marriage does not work, then it does not work. What is the harm in giving it a try?"

"Bhai…" I had no words, I had already entered the trap. No matter what I say I would lose. My brother crafted a flawless trap and no matter how well I argued my point of view, I would not be able convince him until I surrendered to his condition.

"How can you be so cruel Suraj bhai?" I finally said sternly to him, making him aware that I understand his game plan.

"I am not being cruel, it's a fair deal. You want them to be with you, healthy and happy; and I know staying with their unmarried thirty-year daughter will never make them healthy and happy. Above all we hardly have any acquaintances in Mumbai and our parents are used to a socially active life."

"Bhai, I will not leave them in a jungle, there will be a full-time nurse taking care of Papa and other domestic support. I will get them connected to social groups there."

"Have you gone mad?"

"Why mad?"

"You think I cannot take care of my parents? Listen, Nisha, I think enough is enough! It is time you leave. We have had enough of you in our house."

"I will not, Bhai, they are my parents and this is my house too."

The discussion had turned into an argument. There was no one to support me. Shreyas kept quiet, he did not want to be dragged into the fight, he probably agreed with Suraj bhai.

"Nisha, I will give you twenty-four hours to think. If you consider us your family and believe in us, then agree to my proposal. I will ensure that the guy will fit into your criteria exactly as you want. If you are not happy in the marriage for any reason, no one will ask you even a single question, you may walk out whenever you want."

"Bhai, you are giving me twenty-four hours to agree to a blind marriage? What makes you even think I would ever agree to it?"

"Nisha, you can say no if you don't agree."

"But how would I know he is my Mr Right?" Again I find myself arguing something silly.

"You can tell me what the criteria is for your Mr Right?"

"Bhai, everyone knows that, including you." I say on top of my voice.

"If you think I am aware of it then why are you getting so worried? I will stick to my words."

"Bhai!" I sigh in dismay.

I see Suraj Bhai giving Roma a victorious look, and then glaring at me while saying, "Only twenty-four hours. After that if your answer is no then you lose on your proposal to take Papa. I will book your tickets back to Mumbai, so that there are no further arguments. It has to be mutual and you are not allowed to put across any more deals to the Chandras. We don't want any more arguments in the house."

"You are blackmailing me Mr Suraj Prakash Chandra."

"You can think whatever you want, Nisha."

"OK, Bhai, let me come back in twenty-four hours," I accept his challenge without really wanting to but I was left with no other option.

I could clearly feel the game changing. Just a few days ago, I was the one in control, manipulating the situation to avoid getting married. Today, I could see them using the same strategy against me, to the extent that they are willing to send me back to Mumbai, my work life, which mom wanted me to leave so I could come back home.

You usually have plan B in place when plan A fails in the corporate world, but real life is not that generous. It can be cruel and leave you stranded in your own home.

****

Twenty-four hours usually passes quickly but time seemed to have slowed to a crawl. I still do not know how I failed and so miserly.

Did I make a mistake by initiating that discussion? I am actually in a deep ditch now. I can't back out since I proposed to take Papa to Mumbai for his health and Bhai smartly put his condition to tie me. If I reject his condition then I become a villain and if I accept it, then I become a fool. My trust, faithfulness, and love for my family are being tested by my own brother.

He has left me with no option. I cannot say 'No'. This is so cruel of him.

Oh God, why things are getting so complicated. This headache will now go on for another twenty-four hours. Where is the music that keeps me emotionally charged at the time of crucial decisions?

I can't take it anymore. This decision is not about me. Since it is no longer about my happiness, what bother waiting for twenty-hour hours?

Evening

Upset with her situation, she goes to her brother to re-open the topic but he refuses entertain her.

The whole family is glued to the TV enjoying their favourite actor Amitabh Bachhan, who was giving his best performance in the film *Satte Pe Satta*. Prakash Chandra, a die-hard fan of Hema Malini, calls Dhara by that name whenever she is angry. Seeing them having fun, Nisha could not gather the courage to restart the unpleasant topic.

She sits on the stairs and watches the movie without actually watching it. She sees Suraj heading towards the kitchen to get a water bottle. Taking advantage of the opportunity, she approached him.

"Bhai, I need to talk to you?"

"Nisha, come join us for the movie," he says, ignoring my words.

"Bhai, please listen to me."

"If it is about the subject for which you are given twenty-four hours to consider then NO. It's not even six hours since our discussion. Tomorrow, Nisha. If it is about anything else, then tell me what is it?"

"Bhai, I want a fair deal."

"What fair deal?"

"Nothing. I will talk to you in twenty-four hours."

"Sure Nisha"

I am not going to lose at any cost. I have always won in competition with Suraj Bhai, be it chess, cycling, race or tennis. Despite him being the state champion and me an average player, I won. I know love for his little sister, played a major role in my success, and this time too I will ensure he gives up to make me win.

Upset, she goes back to her place on the stairs, next to which was a wooden cupboard which had all the goodies that Dhara made for her children when they were young.

Of all the kids Nisha was seen the most hanging around the cupboard, since she was short no one would guess it was she who stole the goodies. Entire blame would go on to Suraj and Nisha would see him get beatings from their mother.

Suraj knew the culprit but he would continue to remain silent despite the beatings. After a beating session, there would be a melodramatic brother-sister scene in the backyard. Nisha smile to herself thinking about

the old time. The cupboard stands tall as a witness to her mischief and their sibling bond.

As the film nears its end, the family gets excited seeing two Amitabh Bachhan in the same frame, this excitement carries the same freshness, as it would have had when they saw the movie for the first time. The Chandras sat fixed till the end of the movie, Roma actively participated in the family event. The film ended bringing smiles to Chandras. They all chanted, *"chain kuli ki main kuli ki chain"*. Prakash tried to raise his voice but Dhara hushes him, since he was still not supposed to strain.

Silently Nisha observed the efforts each one in the family was taking to make the environment happy for the head for the family. But she knew that treatment from a good place would help a lot more. She had already spoken to renowned doctors of Mumbai and sent them the reports for a second opinion. Since it was a minor attack, things still were under control. A bypass wasn't possible in this state, but there were other treatment options. Thanks to advancements in technology.

She knew what was going on in everyone's mind. They were just praying for many more years of togetherness. Hiding their tears, they all laughed through the fear and pain. Only the ones connected through heart would understand the feeling. It needed no words.

I know that Bhai will not agree to me, and for their efforts my surrender is not my defeat. If I can take Papa along, only on that condition then I agree, I'll give in, once he is fine I can easily walk out of the marriage drama if it doesn't work. Who is going to force me then?

****

Twenty-four hours later.

You should have taken more time to be sure of your decision Nisha. If you tell Bhai that you will get married to the guy of his choice, you will no longer have an option. You know Bhai is from Bhishma Pitamaha category. Once a commitment is made it is final. He will make sure that I stick to my words.

Bhai looks so calm and composed compared to my internal conflict.

"Nisha, sit down."

"Bhai…"

"Listen to me first."

"Sure." I know there is no other option.

"Nisha, I know your concerns, you don't have to be worried about the choice. The guy will be from Mumbai, he will have no objections with you building your career, he will be humble and doing well in his career. He will love and respect your family as much as you do. He will not be a chauvinist. He will definitely not be from our caste so you can boast that your family is not conservative. He will be understanding and above all a good human being. He will be well-read, well-travelled, but with no intentions of settling abroad. He will look good, know how to cook, have his own house, cars and servants. Of course, most importantly, he will be six feet, so you don't have to worry about the height of your kids," he takes a pause. "I find it so funny, Nisha, you have thought about such things. I thought looks and materialistic things don't really matter to you. We were not brought up that way," he says teasing me. I reply quickly so he does not misunderstand my requirements.

"Bhai, it's not about being materialistic, I earn enough. Enough to take care of two families but I know the concerns of Mom and Papa. Despite my marriage they would still feel answerable to our relatives unending list of questions. Finding a man that fits my criteria within our caste is next to impossible. Even if we find one, I'm sure he would not agree to a marriage where we split the cost of the expenses equally. I want us to bear the cost of the wedding not Mom and Papa.

I want a man who is not only good-looking but also earns a lot, because I don't want Mom and Papa listening to the gossip that Prakash Chandra compromised on his daughter's marriage because she was turning thirty," I say all this as calmly as possible.

Suraj looks me in surprise.

"Bhai if you make me agree to your conditions, in order, to take Papa nearer to better health care facilities then you need to agree to all my conditions. I have never compromised in life and never will. Bhai, I trust you and I know you will never let me down. I promise to marry the person of your choice as my love for my family is greater than anything else."

Bhai could sense the tension in my mind. To my surprise, he brings up a silly incident from our childhood, to mellow down the intensity of the situation. I knew it was very much intentional.

"Nisha you have still not changed baby."

"What do you mean bhai?"

"Your list of criteria was there even when you were thirteen."

"Meaning?"

"I still remember hitting Shantanu, the poor guy who proposed you in school after the eighth class exam results were out."

"Bhai please, we are not talking about that." I warn him.

"Of course we are little sis. You had said to him - 'even I like you Shantanu but there is no match between us.' Poor guy did not understand what match you are talking about. You complained to me and I gave him a tight blow. When I spoke to you at length the truth came out. Your percentage did not match and that is why you rejected him and then, had him beaten up by your elder brother. You know what Nisha, I still pity him"

"Bhai please stop it." I just did not want him to say another word about that stupid teenage incident but he continued while laughing his heart out.

"And that huge gap was merely 4.8%. You got 92%, stood fifth and the poor guy got 87.2%, stood twelfth in class. What a great difference."

I turn red with embarrassment. Thank god there was nobody around.

"Bhai please, it was definitely a huge gap. I scored in 90's and he was still in 80's. I was in first ten and he was in first twenty. I repeat there was no match or no scope of going ahead with him." I leave in irritation.

****

Suraj has accomplished the first stage of his plan. He was aware of the most lucrative part of the deal, basis which Nisha agreed. If the guy does not fit into her expectation, he would let her walk out of that marriage without any question. It was tricky but important to get her to agree to the deal.

Nisha gave her consent and walked off. The news that Nisha agreed to marry the guy of their choice reached her parents and everyone was happy. Their parents unaware of the deal between the siblings.

****

Papa comes to my room after bhai disclosed my consent to the family. I am sure he must have played his trick while repeating the conversation.

"Nisha, we hope you are not taking this decision for us."

"No, Papa, believe me, I am getting married because I want to."

"Do you have anyone in mind or you want us to search for the right man?"

"I don't have anyone in mind, Papa."

Papa smiles and says that he will start afresh.

I am so happy to see him happy and relaxed. Just wonder

which route they will take to search for the groom - **for my blind marriage**.

Will they go back to their original style of on-ground activation, personal relationship marketing, word-of-mouth publicity and reference marketing or will they choose the more recent innovative and most trusted style of groom search of our generation—the online *shaadi* portal. Off late, these portals have been claiming about fixing more durable and everlasting marriages than ever.

Their claim seems more promising than the *shaadi pandits* themselves, who would do matchmaking based on the horoscope. It seems like the online space is going to soon eat away the real world and we would all exist on a virtual platform. Virtual marriages, virtual parents, virtual children, virtual friends, virtual relatives and virtual ghosts.

If I continue worrying about how they would locate the perfect match, I would go insane and might end up running away, so let me try and put the marriage drama out of mind.

Unfortunately, I couldn't escape my fate for long. Within two days, Roma enters my room with a big grin on her face. Roma had been spending time with Papa gathering profiles, so he could shortlist them and finalise Mr Right for me.

Well, Miss Chandra, "Do you want to take a look at the lucky man who won your hand? He is a handsome guy, come take a look at his profile."

"And where did he land from, Roma?"

"From a *shaadi* portal."

"I thought as much. A real man drops in from a virtual world and becomes my Mr Right."

"He is the perfect one Nisha, I can guarantee you. Do you want to see?"

I look at Roma in dismay and beg.

"Roma please, I promised Bhai that I would say 'yes' without even seeing the guy. Why did you bring his profile to show me?"

"Nisha, the choice is still yours. Your opinion will always be important for us. Don't ever think that we will force anyone on you."

"Please, Roma, for Mom and Papa, any guy is good for me irrespective of him not being my choice."

"No, you are wrong, Nisha. If they thought any guy would do, they wouldn't have given you so many choices or time to decide. They would have just got you married off. Think back and remember of all your friends who got married without having any choice. Most of them have happy lives and are living without regrets."

"They don't have any regrets because they were never given a choice to think beyond one joker."

I have never thought about anyone beyond your brother, do you think even my choice is wrong?"

"My brother never gave you a reason to look at anyone else, Roma, I know him very well."

"Look Nisha I don't want to argue with you. Are you serious about your decision to get married? Or should I tell your parents that you changed your mind? If you don't want to get married, now is the time to tell us. I don't want to be blamed for the choice you have made. I finally understand why your family is so scared of your decisions and actions. What should I tell your parents?"

I was surprised by Roma's stern tone and behaviour. She almost shocked me, I had to calm her down else she would spoil everything.

"Oh, Roma, please I really like you and I want to have a good relationship with you. I am sorry."

"It's OK, Nisha. We don't have to discuss anything, but I do need to know what to tell your parents."

"Yes, I agree to marry him, and seriously I just don't want to know anything about him, please give my consent to Papa and Bhai."

"OK, and don't worry," says Roma.

"I am not worried, Roma,"

She goes to inform my family about the development and my mom gets extremely excited.

I feel like talking to her, but I am afraid of making a mistake that could spoil the environment in the house.

The guy's family is informed; his mother is from the same city and a small *rokka* ceremony is performed two days after her consent. Technically on this occasion the girl does not meet the guy.

Nisha's parents brought her Mr Right, right out of the virtual world and fixed him into her real life. He was now a dream that actually existed in some part of Mumbai, had his own car, house and earned more than Nisha. He would not demand dowry, share the wedding expenses and would love and respect her family as much as she does. She was also informed that this proposal had reached her father few years ago but at that time, on hearing it was a Mumbai guy, she had refused to consider. No one knows why?

Nisha was sure that the proposals that don't go forward have a reason behind them. She didn't want to upset anyone so keeps quiet about her apprehensions about the acceptance of this, 'once rejected proposal'. Her ego does not allow her to find answers to many questions.

Why was he still unmarried? Am I getting married to a loser? Have I succumbed to a situation that will turn my life into a disaster? What should I do?

Should I speak to Roma?

No, No! I need to sort this battle myself.

I don't know how Roma is so giving. If I were just half as nice, my parents would have been the happiest ones in this world. I'm sure her parents must be upset about her relationship with a man who will not get married until his family issues get resolved. What if our family issues don't get resolved ever? Her parents must be terribly worried; after all she is almost two years older than me.

I feel like the unspoken problem in our home. Nobody talks about it but suffers because I have ambitions.

The guy who is chosen for me could prove to be Mr Right.

Maybe, like me, he couldn't find the right girl of his calibre?

I need to form a positive frame of mind about this marriage, but I don't know how. May be I just need to accept this situation, as it allows me to take care of our parents. I should call up the office and enquire about the company accommodation. It will make it easier for Chandra's to move to Mumbai quickly. I should also call up Karishma and inform her that she has to find a new flatmate as soon as possible. It is time for us to part ways finally. It's sad but having my family there will more than make up for the change.

****

Nisha was lost in her thoughts when Roma came into the room to talk to her again.

"Nisha, are you sure about going ahead with this marriage."

"Oh yes, Bhabhi dear, as soon as possible. I need to get everything sorted. I will fix dates for Papa's treatment with the doctors. They will need to stay with me for not less than a year."

Roma is just too much. I want to hurry things along, while she drags things out by questioning my decisions.

"What? I am talking about your marriage with this guy Nisha. Do you believe that he is your Mr Right," she asks as if she wants me to think again and give Bhai a chance to take charge of the situation.

"Yes, Roma, he is my Mr Right."

As I say this, she looks at me weirdly as if she can't believe my words.

I am sure Bhai must have not spoken about our deal, else she would have made a different level of assumption altogether.

"So you agree, Nisha."

"Yes, Roma, I agree and you may have that in writing unless you don't want me to get married," I said sarcastically hoping to stop her irritating questions that remind me that I was a fool who was trapped in her brother's plot.

I know Bhai loved reading Shakespeare as a teenager and his favourite was 'The Taming of the Shrew'. I will definitely give him the answer when the right time comes. Mostly I have heard of siblings fighting for parental property or to dump parent's responsibilities on each other. I am sure ours must be a rare family where a brother and sister are fighting to take sole responsibility of our parents without any monetary interest.

Well, I still need to answer the list of questions from my darling brother's soon-to-be wife.

"Do you know his name, Nisha?"

"No," I reply curtly, hoping she would get the message.

I don't want to change my mind, you stupid woman.

"Do you want to know?"

"No! Roma"

Why does she not understand? Why am I surrounded by weird characters? My mother isn't enough, now that I have to deal with her soon to be daughter-in-law. The Chandras will have a gala time together. God save our family from everyday arguments.

"What? Why Nisha?"

"He is my Mr Right, dear Roma and that name is enough, I don't want to know anything beyond that." I smile at her.

The moment Papa recovers, he will be Mr Nobody in my life. I will in any case be staying with my parents, since they need me and he is expected to respect them. He has a home of his own in Mumbai with a tiresome job as mine, rather a more tiring job; he won't care what I do. Our marriage won't work and we will walk out of it with mutual consent. The plan is set in my mind, let's see what Mr Suraj Prakash Chandra has in his mind. I know I will beat you in this race, my dear brother. There is no race that you won while competing with me.

"His name is Samar, Nisha. Papa shared your number with him as he wants to talk to you. He will call you to talk about this marriage."

"Does he want to say 'no' to the marriage, Roma?"

God, I wonder if he will complicate things. In the whole game against my brother, I forgot about this angle completely. After all that, there was another person involved, he surely must be having his own philosophies of life. He might have arrived from a virtual platform, but he is very much human, which means a bundle of his own complexities.

"No, not that way, he just wants to confirm that you are happy with what's happening?"

Ah, I sighed, there is someone in this world, who cares about my feelings. I still have time to face the challenges thrown by him.

"I don't want to talk to him, Roma. I am scared that if I talk to him, he will give me a reason to say 'no'. I don't want to get into a situation where my actions affect my family's happiness."

I hope that helps me avoid the route of complexities.

"What do you mean? You want to say 'no' after all the marriage preparations are done?"

I felt like yelling at her. Stupid woman! If I want to change my mind, who is she to stop me? I am trying hard to stick to my words, which is why, I want to avoid any conversation with him. I wanted to scream at her to get out, and stop pushing me into a negative frame of mind, but I didn't. I looked at her quietly, hoping she would get a hint and go away.

When she didn't, then I was forced to say,

"Are you kidding, Roma, why would I do that? Marriage is a lot of investment, and I don't let any project once taken in hand fail at my cost."

"Nisha, your statements scare me. As a psychiatrist and counsellor, you worry me. I can read between the lines, and I am praying I am reading this situation wrong."

"Roma, please don't start using your behavioural science here. Just imagine the level of stress I am going through."

I silently beg her to get out of my room.

"Which is why I can't discount your words, sweetie."

"OK, please tell Mr Samar that I agree to marry him irrespective of what, who, where and however he is."

I join my hands and plead before her. Yes, she is a difficult woman. And it is tough to deal with her.

"But he just wants to talk to you, Nisha."

"I don't want to talk to him Roma, please try and understand."

"No worries, I will ask him to only text you. At least try and reply his messages."

I stare at her in dismay. I surrender.

"OK, as long as they don't provide me with a reason to run in the opposite direction." I say shamelessly.

"Don't worry, they won't. He is a nice guy. You will be happy about your decision."

"Hmm..."

Chapter 8

Then began the journey of **whatsapp courtship** with a person who landed into my life through a virtual platform—a marriage portal. I still wonder if they manufacture Mr Right or customize him as per the bride's requirements. I just hope he is well trained, to at least last till the time I need him. Later I am fine even if he is dismantled and transferred back through the platform that brought him to me.

****

Early the next morning, Nisha's phone beeps.

Hi, thanks for accepting my proposal, Ms Chandra.

Whatsapp message from an unsaved number. Let me check.

Display Picture (DP) – bouquet of roses.

Display Status (DS) – Waiting for her

Display Name – nothing

I know this is the latest Mr Right, but I am definitely not going to respond to the message.

I do not expect a reply. I just hope you are not being pressurised into this marriage. If not, then your reply

is not required, but if yes, then request you to please revert.

He is trying to be smart, as if it would make a difference to my life. I feel like texting him just to say – *'Dude, don't try to be what you are not. I am fine with my decision, as long as you behave well.'*

I don't remember receiving or rejecting any proposal of a man named Samar, but six years is a long time. I know the reason I rejected most proposals at that time. It's surprising; Mom and Papa did not push his profile like they do for every other eligible guy. I am sure his proposal must have come when I broke up with Kabir. At that time, I had decided to never get married, but take another job and shift abroad. I didn't even want to stay in Mumbai.

Kabir...my past. It's so difficult to even imagine that once I was so in love with him. It was a crucial point of my career, and I should have focused on my work instead of having a romance with Kabir. If I ever tell anyone that he almost convinced me to leave work and look after the domestic affairs, no one would believe me. The fact that he had so much influence on me, continues to make me feel stupid till date.

It's been over two weeks that I am home; couple of mails every day but no major trouble. People in Mumbai are very understanding that way. They let you enjoy downtime.

Let me put my mobile aside and sleep.

****

Dhara was affected by her daughter's behaviour. Nisha was not usually quiet at home. She normally chirps around from morning to evening trying to complete past conversations and catch up on the family news. The only time Nisha is seen quiet is when she is disturbed.

Dhara knew whatever was happening was for Nisha's own good. It was difficult not to comfort her and let her off the hook. Dhara knew she had to stay silent and distant if she wanted a better future for her child. Even a momentary lapse of kindness would give Nisha the leeway to change her mind.

Dhara did not want Nisha to reject Samar's proposal at any cost, but at the same time, she was worried about her daughter's feelings and future. She hadn't been in favour of Samar or the proposal six years ago as he didn't have a typical upbringing. She hadn't been disappointed when Nisha had rejected his proposal without a thought. Samar had a good career, was sensible, sensitive and down to earth, but she was still scared of the problems that Nisha might have to face. She didn't want their life, marriage and future to be affected by Samar's sensitive and Nisha's strong-headed nature.

"Do you really think Samar will be able to keep my daughter happy?"

"Why Dhara, what is the problem? Why do you think she won't be happy?"

"You know he was brought up in an unusual environment."

"A good thing, given your unusual daughter."

"What do you mean Chandraji?"

"Dhara, try and understand how he is brought up is not important, who he is now, is important."

"But he was brought up by a single parent. His father left his mother when he was very young. I don't know if he even knows the importance of a family. We have made sure that Nisha met the most distant cousin on earth, while Samar hasn't met even his real maternal uncle, as his grandfather cast his mother out for having a love marriage."

"That was a different time, Dhara, this is a different time. Your daughter and Samar are getting into an arranged marriage, what do you have to say about that?"

"But you don't understand, Chandra*ji*, Nisha is very independent, she takes big decisions of life on her own. It will not be easy for anyone to mould her. Samar is very sensitive, why don't you understand?"

"Dhara, when I met Samar's mother for the first time I got to know that she was in *Jaanki jiji*'s class, in college. She participated in a lot of social work projects, including - the girl child education project. It was during this project that she fell in love with a co-worker, Ravi Samar Singh—Samar's father. Their knowledgeable articles were published in the newspapers. They were celebrities of the town. They both were intelligent and made a good couple. The entire town knew that they were made for each other, but her family was against this marriage since he was from a different caste and not from Nagpur. Against her parent's will, she decided to marry for love.

What happened later is destiny. She is a sensible person. She will make Nisha the best mother-in-law. She won't ask your daughter to change. She would neither ask her if she knows how to cook nor would she expect her to wear saris to please her. She will encourage Nisha to become a better person. We could have not got anyone better than Samar for Nisha. Had I met him eight years ago, I would have agreed to this relationship at once.

Samar is a sensitive person who respects his mother, cares for her and is responsible enough to have taken charge of the family at a very young age, unlike our own boys who feel that their father can buy them the world."

"Now, Chandra*ji*, please don't start that all over again, my sons are good."

"Why are they good, what have they done to make you feel that they have become responsible, Dhara?"

"Don't get overexcited else you will feel tired."

Dhara knows that her husband is a good judge of character. So, she decides to let the argument subside and trust in his decision for their only daughter.

****

While Nisha's parents found their peace, Nisha was struggling to cope with the situation.

The phone beeps early in the morning, disturbing her restless sleep.

I am on leave, why people don't understand. Why are they messaging me so early in the morning?

Good morning, Ms Nisha.

Aha! So this one is from my latest could-be Mr Right.

DP - Boy with a box of chocolate kneeling in front of a girl

DS - Hopeful

I am all smiles, now someone is trying to impress me. I want to reply, but can't get myself to type a message. There are still doubts about him in my mind.

Why am I doing this? Next month, I will get married to him. If this is how I am going to play with life, then the devil in me will take over again and not stop until I screw up everything. I need to delete the thoughts that could cause me to do something I regret.

First thing, I should get out of bed.

Roma wakes up earlier than I do. She is so different and responsible. She wakes up for my house. I wake up for myself. She acts like a responsible daughter of the Chandra family, which I never do. I wonder if after marriage, it will be easy to take up the same role in my new house as Roma is taking in Chandra house. At times feel, I won't be able to cope and will be a disappointment to myself and my new family. I get terrified at the thought of how much my life will change in a month's time, if everything continues the way it is going.

To avoid thinking further, Nisha calls Preeti, her best friend. They had planned to go shopping. This would

give her something to do and help her stop thinking about marriage, Samar and the Whatsapp messages.

"Hey, Preeti, Are you coming?"

"Why do you think I wouldn't? I am waiting for you downstairs with Aunty and Roma."

"Oh, let me come down. Good morning! All of you got up early? I thought I would be the first one," I said, jokingly as I winked at Preeti, just to see Mom's reaction.

"Nishu, who do you think wakes you up, every morning?" replied Mom looking at me, Roma and Preeti one after the other, informing us that in our house no one gets up before her.

"Of course, Maa, you are a champ, who can wake up before you," I say, trying to ease the situation and walk out with Preeti.

"Nisha, be back by afternoon, we need to start your wedding shopping soon, there is not much time," shouts Maa, as we leave.

"Sure, Maa I am here for a few more days, we will shop all you want," I reply, and leave the house finally.

Thank God for Preeti. I don't know what I would have done otherwise.

"So, you are finally caught in the marriage web. How long did you think you could escape?"

"Please, Preeti at least you spare me. I am sick of all this. I said 'yes' and want the discussion on the topic to end."

"Oh really, is it that simple to end? Tell me did you talk to him at length?"

"No."

"Why not?"

"I don't know what to say."

"What do you mean?"

"I don't want to complicate the matter by talking to him. I feel the 'yes' is enough to keep things uncomplicated until I change my mind."

"What do you mean now?" Preeti raises her eyebrows, as if to warn me not to even think of any mischief.

"Nothing, I am just kidding," I try to escape from the conversation, keeping my strategy to myself.

"Talk to him, Nishu. You may want an uncomplicated life, but it doesn't give you the right to complicate somebody else's in the bargain. You may not care if he is your Mr Right, but at least let him decide whether you are his Ms Right. He should have equal right to say 'no' if you are Ms Wrong, shouldn't he? You must reply to his messages even if you don't want to talk. Let him get to know you and if he wants to talk, then allow him the opportunity for him, not for you."

"Preeti, they say I rejected his proposal five or six years ago, and if I did then there must be some reason. He probably is not my Mr Right, but I still agreed to the proposal," I said trying to justify myself.

"Nisha, we are no longer kids. You should know by now

nobody is perfect, not even yourself. Your arrogance will end up destroying him and your family. Don't play tricks. You will end up losing everything if this marriage is nothing but a corporate trick for you."

I am getting irritated with the attitude of my near and dear ones. All of this is making me feel suffocated. My childhood friend is criticising me, just like my beloved brother. I want to ignore Preeti but I just cannot not. Not because it would be rude, but because she is an integral part of my life. She is from one of those few people, who supported my decisions without any doubt. She helped me stay strong and determined, when I decided to move far away from home to the ruthless corporate world of Mumbai. I would call her, disconnect after the first ring and she would call me back. We would play the game - missed call-missed call. She would listen to me for hours when I needed someone to talk to. She would fight with her mother for those extra hundred bucks that she would spend only in listening to me from Mumbai.

Silence reigned in the car as both of us, pondered over our friendship and the discord between our thoughts.

I finally broke the silence.

"Don't get me wrong, Preeti, I will not talk to him, but I have already agreed to text him. Just don't bring this up at home, everyone is already tensed and stressed. Promise me, please."

Both of us smile at each other as it reminds us of the old innocent days and hundreds of God Promise secrets.

I convince myself to reply to Samar. He had been polite and hasn't got offended despite the lack of replies from my side. Had my messages been ignored, I would have automatically added him to the reject list.

I will not start up any fresh conversation but I will reply to his messages politely. I really hope my replying to Samar's messages would end all the doubts.

****

Returning home turned out to be painful. There were guests all over the house. Some had come to meet papa, while others had come to congratulate mom. I was forced to greet most of them and make small talk. Sudden guest arrivals irritate me. It happens only in small towns like Nagpur. In Mumbai, no one dares to come to your place without a prior confirmation. Time is so important!

But seeing mom happy, I relax, at least, she can now make her list of guests, who will return all the gifts she had given for their children's wedding. These barters make me feel like I am a part of some ancient civilization.

I finally escape to my room. Let me text Samar.

Hi

There is no reply for a while and then there is a beep, I jump to read the message.

My excitement fades when I see it's not his message but a stupid life preaching forward from some random acquaintance. It's so ridiculous when people use such silly tricks to connect with you without work.

As I wait impatiently, I save Samar's number and assign it a special message tone. I also check to see if he has read my message.

Two blue ticks – yes he has read.

Is he online – No he is not.

What is this guy up to? Let me check his profile.

DP - Image of a guy in meditation

DS - Thinking.

This is what is keeping him occupied.

But why is he not responding? I don't think I have given him any reason to not reply. How much will he think? Sometimes I am really amazed at the way people behave. Is he the only guy left on earth? What an attitude he has! Is this the way to behave with the girl you are about to marry!

Nisha keeps getting more upset and starts fabricating reasons for the lack of response. She never even considers if he has a similar reaction to her lack of response.

Her phone beeps with the specially assigned tone, breaking the tension.

Hi, Ms Nisha.

You don't have to call me Ms Nisha.

I like it that way.

As you wish. Need to go. Catch you some other time.

I am just not sure of this conversation. I really feel that something is not right. Guess I am still not prepared for this conversation.

It feels as if I am ditching someone. Samar will be my husband and I am preparing myself to be committed to this alliance but it seems as if I am leaving something behind... Something or someone very precious.

I tried to strike a conversation with Samar but failed miserably, now how do I find out if he is well aware of me. Let me check with mom - if he knows how I look like, else he will feel cheated on the day of marriage. I agreed to a blind marriage, not him.

"Mom,"

"Yes, Nishu."

"I need to ask you a few questions."

"About?"

"About this guy."

"Which guy?"

"Maa, this person whom I am going to marry, what's his name?"

"Samar. Nishu, please don't behave like this."

"Yes, Maa, my to-be husband, Samar."

"What do you want to know about him?"

"I don't want to know anything about him. I just wanted to check if he knows enough about me. Does he know about my height, my complexion, my spectacles, my life, my career, our family? Have you shared with him my photograph?"

"We have told him the best we can about you. I don't think we told him that you are tall. We described you as short and dark."

"Mom, is that any way to describe your own daughter?"

"What do you mean? We described you the way you are."

"Mom, sometimes you really make me wonder if I am your real daughter or you guys picked me up from a roadside dustbin. Please ensure that he does not comment on my appearance on the day of marriage. I have faced many funny questions from the so-called prospects in the past. And I will kill him on that day itself, if he embarrasses me."

"Mind your language Nishu. You never reached the marriage hall with any of the prospects we introduced you to. I rather find your reasoning silly. We wanted to share your photograph with him, but we only have your school photographs. And, need I mention that why we don't have your current pictures?"

"Mom, please don't lie. I know you have my pictures."

"Where? In this age, when taking selfies is a craze my daughter does not even click one, let alone allow anyone else to click her."

"Mom, I am talking about those cropped photographs that you took from Preeti's album. The photographs that you gave to parents of that US guy. When we realised both of us had different ideologies, I asked him to return my photographs. Has he not done that?"

"You are talking about those stupid photographs? Do you think they are even worth sending?"

"Why not? Do you think I have changed a bit after that? Don't I still look the same – short, dark, at times with glasses, and above all with my boring black straight hair?"

"Nisha, I am extremely thankful to his parents for their patience. The drama that you created on the very first meeting was pathetic. We never had the courage to fix another meeting with them."

"Mom, listen, if you are going to lie and trick me into meeting random people for marriage, despite being aware of my life priorities, how can you expect me to behave. It's a betrayal! That sudden introduction was such a shocker, and that idiot had failed class 12th, I don't know how he reached to the US. I hate losers and you know that very well."

"This is not how we brought you up, Nisha. We both know who is good at lying."

"Mom, please don't take that emotional route. You have brought us well and that is the reason both you and Papa are happy and proud parents. I can give you a list of children who literally make their parents spend their life crying. And I don't lie, you guys refuse to understand me."

The situation was getting quite intense, Roma wanted to intervene but did not want to spoil her recently formed good image in front of the family, so she ran to find Suraj and asked him to calm them down. Suraj immediately races down.

"Nisha, Maa, please stop. Papa is not well and all our focus needs to be on him, instead of arguing on petty things. We are all responsible for his health, so please be quiet. Nisha I have warned you, not to cause any more trouble. If you want to live your life independently, without any interference from our family, please go back to Mumbai right now and don't bother coming back."

"Bhai, please, I did not start this conversation. I just came to ask mom if all my details are given to Samar. Even if I don't want to know about him, he has the right to know about me. But Mom took the conversation to a different level."

"Don't worry, Nisha, he is well aware of you, and if there is any problem between the two of you, get me involved. Did he speak to you?" Bhai answers to me sternly, as if I am some culprit.

"No, Bhai, we have decided to interact only through messages."

"Why?"

"Bhai, please don't start it all over again. You know the reason. As the mastermind of this drama, you can't act innocent. Let me handle it my way, trust me, I will not let our parents down."

"You are not doing us a favour Nisha. It's a fair deal and you know that very well. It's for your own good, so be sensible in your conduct with him. Any complaint from him and then you watch what I do."

"Bhai, you are warning me?"

"Yes, I am warning you."

Mom sensed something fishy in our conversation, we had kept our deal a secret. Mom is mom, she intervened, forcing us to fabricate another story.

"What deal are you talking about?"

Bhai tried his best to cover up the conversation. "Nothing Maa, I was just delivering Ranveer Singh's dialogues and prompting her to say Priyanka Chopra's dialogues from the movie *Dil Dhadkane Do*. It's a nice film with some interesting conversation between brother and sister."

"Yes, Maa, you know how your kids are, we love talking films. So don't worry," I supported bhai.

Mom gets irritated at us and leaves the room, and we get a chance to discuss the issue at length. Roma's presence doesn't bother us.

"Bhai, why are you behaving like this? Why have you changed so much?"

"I don't want to discuss this anymore, Nisha. Everything is happening as per your wish."

He winds up the conversation and leaves the room making me feel like a fool. My own loving brother has become worse than a strict school principal. We grew up together. We had so much fun together. He was the one I could always rely on. He was the one to encourage me to pursue my dreams. This is why his behaviour more than anyone else's hurts so much. It feels like my entire family has joined hands to plot against me.

This thought circles my mind again and again. I don't want to marry Samar, but I don't have the courage or the freedom to say that aloud. Any sign of doubt is met with reproach and threats to be cast away from the family. I don't even have a concrete reason to reject this marriage proposal.

I don't know him nor have I met him, seen him, spoken to him enough to judge him.

I have faced similar dilemmas before. Since my childhood, many of the decisions were made based on marriage. In school, papa insisted that I take Home Economics instead of French, not because I love to draw or cook, but so that he could say I am a well-groomed girl, who would make a great wife. I never complained about learning how to cook, stitch, knit or paint, rather I worked hard to excel at each skill to make sure papa was proud.

I was also well aware about the fact that dadu had decided to get me married off before the age of twenty. If I hadn't entered into engineering, I would have been married and had two children by now. Apparently, being in charge of your life and having a successful career is the ultimate act of betrayal. *If I fail to conform, they will write me off from the family.*

I am feeling so alone and friendless in my own house. No matter what I do or say is misunderstood and interpreted as changing my mind; I decide to approach Preeti to help me with the Samar situation.

"Hey Preeti, I tried connecting with Samar but I failed to continue the conversation."

"Why, what happened?"

"There is something within me that says I actually know him. Maybe because they say I have been through his profile in the past but just don't recollect when and how. I don't know where this decision will head."

"Don't worry Nisha. No one knows the consequences of the decisions from beforehand. Be assured of the fact that any decision can be amended at any stage in life. There is only one life and you should ensure that you make your share of mistakes. As long as you are alive, you have the power to experiment with your decisions.

Just relax and enjoy this part of life. For some of us including me it is so boring - I have known my husband for years before we got married, but for you it's so unusual."

"Why unusual, you mentioned yesterday that I should at least check if I am his Ms Right. He is getting a chance to know me."

"As if you really care?"

"What do you mean, Preeti?"

"I know you, Nisha. You are still thinking about interacting with him for you and not for him. I only mentioned interacting with him to ensure that you take a sensible decision."

"You know what, Preeti you remind me of a small town, school-going girl who never grew in life despite of becoming a mother of two kids."

"You are very correct, Nisha, I am not as fortunate as you. There is no shame in accepting myself as a small town, middle-class housewife with a shelved life and narrow mind-set."

"Oh please, Preeti, you are exaggerating."

"You are underestimating things. Honestly, I don't know what game you are playing. To me, your ambitious plans sound like Greek, but yes, I have a heart to heart connection with you and that is what keeps me concerned about you."

"I know, you are far wiser than me, Preeti, and that is probably the only reason I turn to you whenever I need to make a wise decision." I try to ease the tension created by this long conversation.

"Just imagine, Nisha, the story that you are creating could only be heard during our great grandfather's time—a married couple who will grow to know each other only after their marriage. And the twist is that you guys are getting married at an age, when that couple would have gotten their children married."

She could make me laugh in any situation. That is what I love about Preeti."It sounds so funny when you put it that way. I just love your innocence, Preeti."

"Oh come on, Nisha, the serial *Balika Vadhu* reminds me of that set-up, I can imagine you and Samar fighting like Anandi and Jagia when they were young."

"Just shut up, Preeti. We won't fight like Anandi and Jagia. By the way how do you know Samar?"

"I have seen his photo. You took a vow not to see him, not me."

"Very funny."

"Seriously, if you want to know anything about him, you can ask me."

"No, thank you, Preeti. I will ask him directly if I have to."

"Oh good, then just start the conversation dear, what are you waiting for, you don't have to worry about anything."

"You know what scares me?"

"What Nisha?"

"I feel am actually preparing for my funeral."

"Stop it, Nisha. Think before saying such things."

"I mean, I am working on creating a reason to give up my own space and allowing someone to intrude into my personal life and likewise for the other person too. The purpose of life would go for a toss. With two minds, things would become more complicated."

"Oh really, then you put a condition to him, all rights to intrude into his life would be reserved with you, but he would not have any right over your life. If he has the courage to send you the proposal a second time, I am sure he must agree to at least this condition."

"Are you sure, Preeti, you want me to get married?"

"Not until you yourself want to."

"You are too diplomatic, Preeti."

"Not with you, I care for you."

"OK, I will try and have an open and honest conversation with him."

"Go baby, best of luck!"

"Bye."

"Bye darling, take care."

Chapter 9

Preeti is a lovely person, I like her philosophies but I still can't not stop thinking.

I feel like everyone knows what is happening, except me. I don't want to delve into this mystery any more, else I will go mad. I think I will just message Samar and get it over with.

I check his state of mind before messaging.

DP - Man riding a horse

DS - Riding my princess away

I find his subtle ways of attracting my attention super cute, damn intelligent and very very interesting. He bloody knows how to keep me engaged. It makes me feel like he knows me better than I know myself. And yes, he slowly is riding the princess along.

Thank god he is online.

Hi Samar, let me know when you are free.

Oh I get an immediate reply.

Hi, Ms Nisha. I am technically free.

Thanks for your prompt reply.

Pleasure is all mine. Tell me what is bothering you.

How do you know - something is bothering me?

I am quite a devil. I can sense the tension and I am known to increase it further.

The tension is with regards to you, Samar.

You mean you are getting concerned about me, even before our marriage.

No.

I reply promptly with no inhibitions. It is not something that raises a concern.

There is a long silence after my reply.

It seems that my 'No' was taken the wrong way. Again, I have someone, who needs a clarification. I elaborate my point of view, quickly, not wanting to argue with yet another person.

No, I mean, I need to discuss something with you.

Then, I get an immediate reply, as if Samar on the other side was waiting, only for me to give an explanation. Sometimes life becomes so obvious that you can guess what is going on in the other person's mind.

What?

I want to know if you know me enough to agree to this marriage.

Are you sure, that's your question, Ms Nisha?

Pretty sure. Why?

People try to hide things and here you are trying to reveal.

Meaning?

Ms Nisha, your question implies that I will change my mind if I get to know you better.

You may change your mind.

What? Are you getting aligned with the intention of changing your decision?

I am not talking about me, Samar. We are talking about you.

What about me, Ms Nisha?

I am sure you have some picture of your Mrs Right set in your mind. What if I don't match that? Do you know me well enough?

Yes, Ms Nisha, I know you well enough.

How? Did you go through my profile and pictures?

Yes.

Just like others, do you want to meet before taking a final decision?

Do you have any doubts? Are you not sure about your decision?

I am sure.

I am too.

Are you trying to play games with me, Samar?

Are you under any pressure, Ms Nisha?

No, are you under some pressure?

You are not so bad, Ms Nisha that I have to agree to marry you under any pressure.

I feel you should rethink your proposal.

You are free to reject my proposal again, Ms Nisha.

Oh, so you know about that!

Yes, I do.

I thought your proposal reached me by mistake. You must have forgotten about the first one.

What is there to forget or to remember?

You could not find a suitable girl for yourself in these six years?

Just as you could not find a suitable man for yourself.

Don't get personal.

I won't unless you define a space within which we could have our conversation. I feel that we are equal in many aspects—career, family views, personal values etc.

Do you think people with similar attitude can settle together?

Well, Ms Nisha, if one has to find reasons, then there are many to not go ahead with a decision, and many reasons to go ahead as well.

I have no words. I decide to turn off my mobile and close my eyes, before this discussion gets me into some other controversy.

The conversations with Samar did not seem real. Many guys pretend to be good in the first few interactions and later on show their true colours.

Though I don't have any reason to worry. I have already decided on my plan, he is just a temporary addition to my life. This time if I allow a man to enter my space, my life will definitely not get affected, if it does not work out.

And if he actually turns out to be Mr Right, then life is sorted, I will be living with him happily forever.

What if Samar actually says no? Papa's health is more important. I know Bhai will not hold me to our deal. In any case, next week, I am going to meet good doctors in Mumbai. And once they give a green signal, I will take Papa along. I might have to shift my house next month itself based on what they say.

I want to be out of the marriage trap but I will exit this trap with a 'No' from Samar. This would ensure I get brownie points for being as good as possible.

I know it is nothing but the fear from my relationship with Kabir that keeps haunting my mind. It does not allow me the confidence to give anyone a chance to enter in my life.

Samar seems very straightforward. He reminds me a bit of Kishore. We were studying engineering at the same college. We were good friends and our similarities made me think, he was the right one for me. Then he showed his true colours turning every project, every exam, and every task into a competition.

There are days I wish he was my Mr Right—same city, same class, same age, same score and same future career path.

Samar seems familiar that way — same personal views about life and same independent mind-set. Though now my priorities for expected similarities have changed. But I am still worried this would lead to the same competition track. Before it heads anywhere wrong I need to cut this journey off.

Most people go on blind dates and here I am planning a blind marriage. Exactly like how Dadi wed Dadu. They did not meet before marriage nor did they know about each other. Their generation was so different from ours, yet I am on the verge of repeating history.

Nisha goes out for a walk in the evening. Birdie was a famous junk food joint attracting youngsters from different corners of the town.

As a child I used to often come to this cake shop, sitting in front of papa's Bajaj scooter, the most popular family two-wheeler at that time. I would take five pastries in one box and one in a separate box. The separate one would always be kept hidden from Bahi and Shreyas in the tall cupboard next to the staircase. When everyone was out, I would quietly enjoy the special piece, at times feeling guilty about cheating.

As I pass by the shop, exchanging smiles and waving hands at the staff out there, a strange feeling crosses my heart. I am no more that little child, who could shamelessly have the special piece. I am a grown up, responsible adult and expected to behave in a certain way.

As she walks she realises her cell phone was on silent mode and there was a missed call from none other than Kabir. The most unwanted, yet most strongly present character in her life.

Yes, Kabir you will be missed. I just hope, Mr Right proves to be the best decision of my life. The journey from forgetting you to allowing someone into my life is the most difficult part of my life but I am going to walk that path with no regrets.

I should try to have a meaningful conversation with Samar without actually thinking about the consequences. I fear that I am going to screw this relationship even before it starts. And I must get over this fear.

She picks up her phone and reads the entire conversation between her and Samar. She visits his profile.

DP - A cloud sailing across the sky

DS - I know we are made for each other.

I know this message is for me and I just can't stop smiling at his gestures.

No one has ever showered me with this much attention. Technology is amazing. You can connect without being connected. You can discard without even a mention.

Everyone at home is keeping a watch on my everyday activities to ensure that I am following their instructions and here, there is someone, who is leading my thoughts towards him without saying a single word.

He can connect to me. I feel he can read my mind.

Hey, Samar.

Hi.

One serious question.

Are you sure you are serious?

Not always... But right now, yes.

Tell me.

Why did you agree to marry me?

Meaning?

Samar, please I really want to know, how someone can agree to marry a person without even wanting to know or meet.

Just the way you agreed.

Samar, my case is different.

Different? How?

My decision is forced.

Are you serious?

I don't know. They have left it for me to decide and I didn't know what else to do.

You mean you are not interested in this marriage?

I think I am confused about life.

Why?

I have never thought this would happen so suddenly. I thought my search for Mr Right would never end in this life. I have been on this hunt for so many years now, but never came across anyone.

If you are a hunter, do you have a whip to tame your prey?

Hahaha...Now that is funny.

No, seriously, it happens with overly ambitious women. They expect their husband to be obedient. They become more demanding. They start thinking that life is all about money and power— the 'who dominates whom' game.

What do you mean? I don't expect a henpecked husband. I

was trying to share my point of view, but I guess you are chauvinist like all other men.

I wish I had gotten married at twenty—a mindless, obedient drone agreeable to her parents and husband's wishes. I just want to erase the realities of life that I have seen. I want to forget the fact that I have seen people turning bitter after being in love, people betraying their partners, people giving up their lives unable to handle a bad relationship. People who decide to begin a life together and destiny takes them away. I hate the fact that no one wants to accept me as a person I am, all they want is an obedient girl who doesn't have any opinions of her own.

I wish I was back to Mumbai—comfortable and happy. Not forced into the wall of uncertainties where no matter what I do or say, it will be considered wrong.

My phone beeps again getting me back to reality.

I was just pulling your leg Ms Nisha, please don't take it personally.

I did not reply. The phone beeps again.

I am very serious about 'us'. You may find it strange but the reason is very sensitive.

Intrigued, I reply.

What is the reason?

It has to do with my weakness, my mother.

Your mother?

Yes.

Can you please elaborate?

I was brought up in a single-parent household and my mother is very attached to me. She has been through so many tough times and I have seen her struggle unable to help.

I always wanted to give her the happiness she deserves. The day she saw your profile, there was a lovely smile on her face. Both of you grew up in the same city, but she hasn't been able to return to her childhood home due to some harsh decisions.

When I saw her happiness, I decided you are the one for me. I don't know how good a person I am but I promise to keep you happy since you make her happy. Every time she hears of you or talks about you she is all smiles. And I guess it's destiny that brought us back together, otherwise six years is a long time.

I keep on reading his messages, one after another, word after word, and line after line. A man, who loves his mother so much that he agrees to spend the rest of his life with me without even meeting me, must be an amazing man.

I appreciate your sentiment, Samar. I just don't know if I am that good.

Hey, why do you underestimate yourself? I know you are quite good and mature.

How can you say that?

Because you have come a long way.

In your language any ambitious girl could come this way.

All I know is your hard work is clearly visible. You shouldn't doubt yourself just because others are unsure.

How can you say that?

We guys have a sixth sense and we can judge a girl in and out very well in the first conversation itself.

And then treat her the way you want. Don't talk to me like that.

Come on, Ms Nisha, why do you get offended at every sentence? I don't intend to hurt you.

It's a difficult topic. If I were a man my efforts would have been applauded, but since I am a woman I have no dignity, my hard work is dismissed and I am labelled as a control freak and overly ambitious woman.

Please, it's not that, Nisha. I did not mean anything. It was on a lighter note.

The respect is missing, Mr Samar, and I better be called Ms Nisha. That sounds better.

Sure :-) Anything to ensure that you know I respect you.

Yes, that sounds better.

Sure, Ms Nisha Madam.

Goodnight.

I felt a little stupid. I had only argued with him to stop

the conversation about marriage. I assumed that arguing would lead to a big debate and Samar's ego would come into play when challenged. Instead, he was quite submissive.

The only question is - is he submissive, smart or a gentleman? He reminds me of someone. Just wish I could remember who. It's as if he can see all my cards and is able to adjust the game accordingly to ensure that he wins. I must have spoken to him in the past or he is really, really smart.

She goes to sleep, but her sleep is restless. There weren't too many days left for their marriage and she was not sure of the decision she has taken. In an attempt to make her parent's happy she has locked herself into a cage.

She was unwilling to analyse the consequences. She only hope to get some respite from the situation when she was back to Mumbai.

****

The situation at home starts improving. Roma stops staying with us. I have my room all to myself once again. I miss talking to her though. Papa's health has improved. I decide to return to Mumbai and get back into action.

The night before leaving for Mumbai, Papa's old friend, Uncle Sahu, invites me home for dinner. Uncle Sahu is papa's only Bengali friend. His wife cooks delicious non-vegetarian food. I love the elaborate meals that they serve. I always love being invited to their place, even more after Sudha bhabhi, their elder daughter-in-law joined the family. She treats me as her younger sister and that means a lot.

At the dinner table, Sahu uncle starts his usual conversation. The prime focus of his conversation - defend papa (his best friend) from every corner possible, in a self-created verbal argument and then blame me for being irresponsible.

"Nisha, I'm glad you agreed to marry. Samar is a nice boy; I know his mother's family. They are very sweet people. We will also be inviting them for the wedding from our side. Not sure if they would come from Samar's side."

"Uncle, I don't know much about Samar's situation with his family. All I know is that I want to see my family happy. Papa means the world to me." I try to hit the bull's eye and get in his good books from the start of the conversation.

"Yes, Nisha, your father is a gem of a person, but you can't even imagine the societal pressure he has been facing about your marriage. We belong to a conservative society and we try to abide by the systems laid by our forefathers." He just loves to take papa's side, how much ever I try.

"What kind of societal pressure, Uncle? As far as my life is concerned I am doing pretty well in life."

"You will understand that only when you will become a mother."

"But, Uncle I feel society should be happy if someone is doing well for self without harming anyone. And I believe Prakash Chandra and his family have never behaved badly with anyone."

"You did not marry on time. People have been talking about you." This is one topic which I hate discussing. It irritates me to the core.

"Talking? I never heard anything from anyone, Uncle."

"They would never say anything to you, but your father has to face the consequences of your attitude."

"How would their words affect my parents? Why should strangers be more important than their own children?"

"A father who cannot find his little princess a prince is judged to be an incapable person."

"Uncle, he should give his princess time to understand the prince."

"Please, Nisha, your father has given you enough time to know yourself and the guy, now it's high time."

"Uncle, my marriageable age was over ten years back as per society norms. Does it really matter whom I marry and at what age anymore?"

"You are being extremely difficult, Nisha."

"I am not, Uncle. I just want practical answers to my practical questions."

In anger, uncle Sahu shared a piece of information –"Samar's mother is a very nice lady but made the decision to marry for love, disregarding her parent's wishes, and repented for life. She is happy with Samar and your marriage as she can connect back to the society, which she had to leave."

"Uncle, she wants to connect with her family, not to others who made her life difficult."

"You don't understand, Nisha, and I probably am not the right person to explain it to you."

I did not want to spoil the lovely dinner, so I decide not to argue with him further and continue eating. Once dinner was over, I lavish aunt with praises and then go to spend some time with Sudha bhabhi.

Both of us spend time reminiscing about the past.

It was a nice respite for Nisha, who had spent days being smothered by everyone else's excitement of her marriage.

"Nisha, do you remember how much you loved Pooja Bhat's movies as a child. If you count the number of movies she acted in, you will realise there isn't a single movie where she didn't run away from her home. There was always a reason that triggered her to leave home and pursue life. I always believed that like her, you also ran away from home. Your decision to move out of Nagpur was inspired by a deep interest in exploring the 'how'."

"Oh God, Sudha Bhabhi, not again, please. You guys have teased me enough during my childhood. Please not any more, have some mercy, I am a grown woman, and people respect me for my work. Please, please, please... don't mention it ever again, I don't want to give anyone the chance to make fun of me."

I know that Sudha bhabhi wanted to pull my leg a little more, but understanding the gravity of the situation she thankfully remained quiet. I used to love analysing Pooja Bhatt's movies as a child. She is amazing as an actor.

"Don't worry, Nishu, come let me show what I brought for you." She brings in a beautiful suit piece that she bought from Kolkata.

"Wow, Bhabhi, it's so lovely. I like it a lot. Thank you so much."

"This one is for your office, and I have already decided what you are going to wear for the reception. Just let me take your measurements, I will go with Roma and Aunty to get the stuff. It will be a surprise for you. Don't bother about your shopping at all."

I felt overjoyed with this gesture. She is not a part of our family nor is Uncle Sahu, but they are equally concerned about Chandra's happiness. I hug everyone while leaving, even Uncle, to let him know that whatever difference of opinion we have, he would always be my dearest uncle.

Chapter 10

I have flown to-and-fro to Mumbai for past eight years but this is the first time I am listless on the journey. This whole marriage situation has left me feeling heavy with a burden that I can't dispel.

As I settle, there is an early morning message from Samar.

Good morning, Ms Madam, hope I am not too early.

No you, are not, Samar.

Oh, that way.

Meaning?

You want me to call you Madam but you will call me Samar. What about my dignity? Where is my respect?

Felt like laughing, instead I smile.

:-)

You are very smart, Ms Madam.

Hahaha. Why have you messaged? Some work or just to pull my leg again?

To say something I would have to call, but you have blocked my number. I am only allowed to chat with you through these messages. So messaged. Not that I am complaining, but.....since you asked.

You tried calling me? We decided we would not.

You are quite mature and I am sure there must be some sensible reason for such a decision. I did try calling you. Not as mature as you are.... Sorry.

Thank God I did that, else you would have got me into trouble.

No, I called to get you out of the trouble.

What do you mean?

I want you to take some time to decide whether you want to go ahead or not.

Meaning?

I am giving you time to think about your decision to marry me.

Do you need time to think?

No, I only want you to make the right decision. I can't have you forced into this marriage.

Till when I do have the time.

Now that is tricky. You have all the time to reconsider your decision until the day we meet and get engaged, officially.

Are you serious, Samar?

Yes.

Wow, you are dictating terms to me already. I am impressed.

I am just trying to return the good you did.

Meaning?

You started conversing with me because you thought I should know if you are right enough for me or not, similarly I think you should also have that option.

I am impressed.

What is the logic behind this timeline?

If we get married, I don't ever want you to say that I have been unfair to you.

What if I say 'No'?

I will let you go to whomever you want provided you have someone.

What if I fail to say 'No' not then, but later?

You get your chance only till we get engaged, nothing beyond that.

Is that the deal?

Exactly. You may think as much as you want.

Do you even know what you are giving me?

Yes, a chance to live your independence.

What do you think I will do?

You will say 'Yes'.

Are you so sure of yourself?

I am so sure of you. Enjoy your time living your way. If you want to continue talking, I am available, Madam.

Thank you so much, Sir.

I am quite surprised by the entire conversation. I visit and re-visit the complete conversation in an attempt to figure out if there was a catch. Samar seems to be a rare character. He had eased the suffocation and given me room to breathe amidst the stress of my family. I want to thank him, but I cannot get myself to acknowledge his understanding. Is it my ego?

Just before I switch off the phone, I follow my newly formed ritual - visiting his profile.

DP- Guy and girl sitting on a cycle.

DS - Don't get me wrong.

No, Mr. Samar I am not getting you wrong but you are making me crazy about you.

Chapter 11

When Nisha reaches Mumbai, she finds her life changed. She has gained a friend. Someone she can text her problems to. A virtual listener, a reader of her heart and mind, someone who will try to understand her, no matter what. She knew for sure that he wouldn't make any judgments and even if he does, she did not have to give him any explanation. A zero-stress relationship, a rare case in her life.

She found herself mellowing. It was a nice change, but she knew she wouldn't allow this phase to remain forever. Change is the only constant phenomena in life - when, what, how and where need not be questioned.

Samar was a new experience for her and she was trying to find an opportunity to overpower this equation before she was overpowered by the situation.

The fun part of this experience was that at the end of the day, she actually had someone to share her time with. She was happy despite Samar's virtual presence. While her mind still wanted to maintain a distance, her heart mellowed with the gift of expression. She no longer hesitated before texting Samar.

A peep into his profile had now become a daily routine.

There was a box of lovely chocolates, which clearly was for her. It said – For you. Nisha so much wanted to respond - thank you – but did not go ahead. She did not want him to know that secretly she had started pursuing him. Not sure of her feelings, she composes herself and gets back to the agenda with him, after returning from work.

Hi, hope I am not disturbing you Samar

Hey, not at all.

How was your day?

It was good and how about you, Ms Nisha.

Weird, but great!

Why?

I picked a fight with VP of another division. My ex-

boss in fact.

Looks like you are a tough fighter, Ms Nisha.

What do you mean?

Nothing! Just that we all have our ways to deal with things.

Hmm…

When I get into arguments, I only listen. I feel it is better to not get carried away. It takes a lot to lose your cool and get involved into unnecessary fights, but nothing at all to ignore.

I can't ignore it when something is wrong. It just doesn't let me be.

Probably you have too much to prove, Ms Nisha.

I am like that Samar. Just thought I should share my negative side with you, so that you are not unaware if we decide to proceed.

Whatever you think is negative could actually be your strength, Ms Nisha.

I don't think so. Trust me, I get criticised for my attitude - a lot.

The world cannot accept people who have strong opinion, because they can't form one. If someone has one, they either fear the person or fight against the fear of accepting his strength, as they know it would cause them to surrender.

What do you mean by that, Samar?

Nothing, Ms Nisha you think a lot about your action. Just relax, take it easy.

Wish it was that easy for me. I view life differently.

I like the way you deal with it, Ms Nisha.

What do you like about it?

The honesty!

I think I have quite a casual approach towards life unlike others.

I don't think so, Ms Nisha.

Do you know what, Samar, I think am already in love with you.

What?

Don't you think I am being honest, Samar?

No, Ms Nisha, I think you are being too casual about something very serious and precious.

I told you so, Samar, I am very casual towards life. The whole idea of being serious puts me off.

But you have been extremely serious about life.

What makes you say that?

Some are serious about the rules formed by society while some are serious about the commitments towards self. I feel you fall in the second category and that is fair enough.

Samar, I am impressed by your explanation, but I still don't find it convincing enough.

I promise you, Ms Nisha you will understand what I mean some day.

Don't be so overconfident about yourself, Samar. I might be the wrong one.

Challenge?

Yes, Samar. Challenge!

In a blink, our deep but light-hearted conversation turns into a duel of wills.

I could feel different kind of a thrill. I am going to prove my point and this marriage will not materialise. As I type a message, reality strikes, making me realise where the conversation is heading. Finally, I decide to end it there. For the first time in years, I called a cease-fire to an argument, which is so unusual of me.

Hey, Samar, I think I am back to screwing everything. Can we connect tomorrow?

Sure, Ms Nisha. Goodnight and take care.

Putting the phone down I try to regain control. Tired and in two minds, not sure of the future. I don't know why I get so aggressive. There is no reason. There is a marriage agreement between us but instead of getting to know him better I am actively causing misunderstandings unnecessarily.

This poor guy was actually trying to convince me that he does not think there is anything wrong with me. He is ready to accept me the way I am, unlike the others, but I keep poking and aggravating the situation. This is not what I want. I need to get over this madness. I need to stop letting office and Kabir affect my mind.

Kabir, I know there is no one in this world who I could love as much. I know what I am guarding myself against, for so many years. It's you and only you. It's difficult for me to let anyone into the place I once gave you.

****

The next morning as she gets ready for the day, she looks at herself in the mirror.

I feel like a college girl, I smile at my reflection, send a flying a kiss towards the mirror before moving out of the room. Yes, things around me are changing, and for the better. I am sure I will reach a conclusion soon.

What is the need to take routine as a routine, it might turn out to be an interesting day, if not fruitful. People will take time to accept me as a VP, and I need to give them that time, else it will not be fair on my part. After all, could-be Mr Right says that I am honest. Let me prove him right.

She smiles at herself again and collects her stuff from the table.

I have not been to the gym ever since the accident; it's time to get back to the routine otherwise like today I will have to keep skipping breakfast and dinner every day.

On my way to the exit door I hear Karishma call.

"Hey, Nisha, why did you not meet me yesterday?"

"Hey, Karishma, good morning. Sorry, I was too tired."

"I am packing lunch for you. Take it before leaving."

"I am just leaving, Karishma."

"So then take it now."

"Yes, of course. I am coming."

I always hate this wife-like behaviour from Karishma, but today it does not irritate me like usual. Instead, I think only good about Karishma.

She came into my life a few years back when I was looking for a shared apartment in Lower Parel. If it weren't for this apartment, Karishma and her crazy philosophies would not have been a part of my daily life. This woman, who my mother hates, has brought a lot of fun to my life. She was the one who helped me when I had lost all hope from life.

She was the one who pulled me out of the break-up depression. I couldn't talk about Kabir and my relationship with anyone at home. Just when I felt it was time to tell people at home about us, we broke-up. I threw myself into work trying to get over our relationship, but all I did was work and breathe, I had stopped living.

Karishma helped me learn to live again. Like an elder sister, she took care of me. She made me feel like home in this apartment. We were four girls in the beginning and Karishma was my roommate. With time only the two of us remained and our bond grew stronger. She and her stupid life philosophies pushed me to fight back and live.

Now we stay in separate rooms of the same apartment.

****

Before going to the office, I meet the doctor to discuss papa's reports. A bypass is not recommended but his hypertension needs to be reversed and his weight reduced. The doctor suggested a two-month treatment plan but only when, Papa was comfortable to travel. He also recommended at least two months rest for Papa before moving him to Mumbai, which meant enough time for me to settle both at work and with marriage. I know that my fears have no meaning since the objectives are clear.

There is no room to accommodate any more mistakes. Everything has to be perfect and carefully crafted. Above all, I have to maintain the best of my mind-set. I am no longer a free bird. A more responsible Nisha has emerged due to the trials and dramas of life.

A constant reminder of this change is an early morning message from Samar. While I still suffer from moments of doubt and insecurity, I do enjoy having someone who is ready to accept me as I am.

Good morning, Ms Nisha.

DP - A hot cup of coffee

DS - Waiting to have it with you.

I just can't stop but smile. Is he being cute or am I behaving like a teenage girl?

Good morning, Samar.

Falling in love is the most beautiful experience. It happens with everyone and the way it happens makes you feel so special about yourself.

Hope India wins today.

Hope I get time to complete my presentation today. There is an important assignment coming my way.

Ms Nisha, are you serious?

We have discussed this and you approved that I am quite serious in life, Samar.

You must be kidding, Ms Nisha.

Kidding about what? Being serious?

OK, so tell me how you enjoy life, Ms Nisha?

I enjoy life by living it my way, doing all that I want to.

You mean to say that you enjoy life by giving those extra hours of your personal life to your company and making them millionaires.

How do you enjoy your life? By spending a few hours in front of TV watching cricket matches and making those organizers, TV channels and advertising companies' millionaires?

You know six years ago when I was your age, I used to think the same, but not anymore.

Samar, we are at two different life stages. I love watching movies and my entire family avidly follows Bollywood and that is how I enjoy, if that is what you mean by your question.

Hence the difference of opinion. I don't watch movies at all.

I don't know if this would work.

That is not for you to decide alone, I am an equal partner to that final decision.

Samar, why do you talk from both the extremes?

What extremes?

When I try to find reasons to be positive, then you give me freedom of choice. When I feel it might not work then you say that you won't let me take that decision alone.

Did I say that, Ms Nisha?

Samar, what are you up to?

Nothing, I am just being myself.

Samar, it seems like you are more confused than I am or you think you are extra smart.

Please, Ms Nisha, you don't have to misunderstand everything.

I don't think I have any patience left to even think of understanding you.

Let us put a hold to our conversation Ms. Nisha, until you come back to normal.

I am talking sense, Samar. Don't put words into my mouth. Yes, let us put an end to this conversation right now because I don't think this will work out.

It's so annoying.

Continuing this conversation is just not possible. An outsider intruding in my personal life is just not acceptable. I am very much aware of my life. He was mocking me for living a less than full life.

I was angry at him for some time, but after a while, yes, I cheated and peeped into his whatsapp profile.

DP – Blank

DS -Wish she understands my silence too.

I just didn't know what to do. Just as I was struggling to get over my inner battle, there was a knock from my cabin door. It seemed as if it was from within my inner doors. I looked up to see, it was the same man standing in front of me, whom I had argued with, the day before.

Kabir! A tall, handsome man in his mid-thirties blessed with a great deal of charm. When he looks at you with his intense steel grey eyes, you feel like he would sweep you off the floor. His voice is magical—when he starts to talk, he steals the show. It was to him I lost the best presentation award. It was to him I lost my heart, it was to him I was all set to marry, it was for him I agreed to give up my career. There he stands looking at me, adding to my inner conflict and making me feel like quitting everything and pursuing a life of loneliness. With him around, I can never mentally and emotionally move on. His mere presence gives me comfort. Yes, I fight with him, yes I hate him but at the end of it all, I still want to be with him. I could never answer myself why I refused to take up the opportunity of going to the US for work. Instead I came back to Bijals and joined a separate department after our break-up.

In those sixty seconds, I re-lived those two years of my life, which we spent together. Neither of us said a word, but our eyes spoke about all the grudges we were holding against each other. Silence screamed on top of its voice, only to make me realise that I needed a break, a break before it makes me break down emotionally. Kabir, just go please.

"Hi, Nisha, how are you?" Kabir tries to break the tension, jolting me back from my memories.

"I am good, Kabir. Tell me how I can help you," I speak curtly. I hope my eyes convey that I did not want to help him even if I am the only person on earth capable.

"I am not that bad, Nisha, trust me."

"I know you are a thorough gentleman, Kabir, and that is why I have been so polite with you. You were my boss once upon a time and I will always respect this fact."

He smiles and says, "You were a brilliant subordinate, Nisha."

"Thank you, Kabir, for your kind words. They mean a lot. What do you need, Kabir? I need to complete my work. Tomorrow is my final presentation. And if we still have to discuss the two-month old matter which involves my two team members then I just don't want to talk about it. Let Mr Bijal take the final call."

"No worries, Nisha, I just came to invite you for dinner tomorrow."

"Why, is it your birthday tomorrow?" He pauses and then looks at me.

"Oh yes, tomorrow is the May 22, how could I forget."

It is the day I used to celebrate with him when we were together, making him feel the most special person in the world. Post break-up, I celebrate his birthday with Karishma, without even letting her know the reason.

"Nisha, I am on leave tomorrow, but I want you to have dinner with me," says Kabir, despite the fear of rejection.

"Of course, we will all come, Kabir," I reply, pretending an enthusiasm, brushing all the thoughts that were killing me at the back of mind.

"I want to invite you, Nisha. Not the whole team," he says as if he was giving me instructions and I hate that attitude from him.

"I am not your subordinate anymore, Kabir, watch your tone else I will have to raise my voice," I reply in an angry, yet polite way.

"I am sorry, Nisha, I did not want to hurt you, but I really wish to spend time with you," he says.

"I am not getting into the same trap again, Kabir. It's

been six years. Do you really think I will make the same mistake again?"

"Nisha, I have not come to hurt you today, nor did I want to hurt you back then. You have always blamed me for what went wrong, but tell me what exactly did I do wrong? You are the one who is ambitious and keen on proving your merit. You wanted to reach my level.

Well, today, we are both VPs. Maybe in a few years I will get a chance to become a part of the Board of Directors. This opportunity will arrive a few years earlier for me given my seniority, but you too will get that opportunity sooner or later. However, I wouldn't mind giving up such an opportunity if you would at least give me a chance."

"Kabir, you want me to give you another chance to break my heart?"

"No, Nisha, I would never do that."

"Kabir, it took me years to get over that insult."

"Nisha, I wasn't insulting you. You misunderstood what I said. You often misunderstand things and you struggle due to these misunderstandings."

"Kabir, listen I just don't want to argue with you. We were together and now it is over. Yes, I am not as capable as you, but I am where you are and that is enough."

"Exactly what I am trying to tell you. Nisha, let us not fight anymore can we please start again from where we had left off?"

"No, Kabir, it's difficult to deal with your chauvinism. Now, please leave and let me work."

"Chauvinism? Nisha, why do you always connect our personal life to our professional life? There is a clear difference between the two. You won't ever be happy if you mix the two. You have always made that mistake. Do you know that I feel like a loser because of you?"

"A man who cannot respect a woman is always a loser."

"If the woman is so dumb that she does not understand priorities in life, how will he be able to build his life with her?"

"Kabir, you cannot call our life 'ours', if you are the only one in-charge."

"Nisha, when it comes to married life, it is the man who takes the responsibility and the woman who builds the house. I wanted you to be the woman of our house and not the man. This conversation is going nowhere," Kabir says, turning and leaving as I look on.

****

In his cabin, Kabir sat thinking about the time when he was dating Nisha. They were happy together, she meant the world to him, but she never told her parents about their affair. He was ready for marriage, but she wanted to work for some more time. Small achievements in office would make her happy, but Kabir who was a Senior Manager then, thought her achievements were typical of work growth and not a reason to celebrate.

He wanted her to separate personal and professional life, but Nisha couldn't. She was so engrossed in building her professional life that she couldn't see the difference. She was too excited and too immature to strike a balance between the two lives.

This difference in their attitude created a rift between them,

She was serious about him, but he didn't realise that little things made her happy. He would boost about his work and position in the company, but would never appreciate her little achievements. He expected her to resign and sit at home once they were married as she barely made 1/10th of what he earned back then.

She was beautiful, intelligent and more than anything else untouched by the filth of the corporate jungle. He was possessive about her and hated seeing her talk to other men. He wanted her to remain untouched by the horrors of the world and only look after the domestic affairs once they got married. There were reasons behind his actions, which he never mentioned. It reminded him of his childhood time when the woman dearest to him worked like a man to meet the ends of the family.

This conflicting attitude between Nisha and Kabir was the cause of many fights, which ultimately lead to her leaving his life—personal and professional. He did not want her to go but he couldn't stop her nor did she let him speak to her and fix the situation.

He was thankful that, she wasn't gone from his life forever at least not professionally. She left his department, spoke to the VP of HR and got transferred to a different division. She worked from scratch and grew to the level where she was equal to him. He had underestimated the wrong girl. In the past six years, there wasn't a single day when he did not think about her.

He was happy that she had returned. For that one moment, he was ready to give up anything and everything he possessed in life. He thought of talking to her, but Shrija asked him to let her settle first, get to the level where she wanted to be and then approach. He saw her around in the office, even if she avoided him as far as possible.

Six years passed, yet every conversation with her gave him a feeling like no time had passed. She was still very angry. The only satisfaction for him was that she hadn't found anyone who could make her happy just like he hadn't.

I hope one day soon, she will realise, that work can never take the place of your personal life, the moment it does you become nothing but a machine that does not need a heart to feel. I tried to explain this to her, but she was too stubborn to accept.

As he reminisced about their past, Nisha continued doing her work, she got her presentation approved and left for the day. On her way home, she thought about Kabir.

Kabir is a part of my past. He never respected my dreams.

I never dreamt of becoming a VP but I dreamt of living my life with him. My career defines me, but he thought that I was incapable of handling anything in life. He wanted to talk to Mom and Papa, who would have either agreed to everything that he said and married us off at once or would have forced me to return to Nagpur. As it is they weren't thrilled with my move to Mumbai and to add to it a love marriage would have been too much for them to take. I did not want to end up living an incomplete life.

****

Chapter 12

I don't feel like having dinner let me at least talk to mother. I haven't spoken to her since I got back, which is quite unusual. I am now in constant touch with Roma to get updates on papa's health.

"Mom, hi, sorry my phone was on silent. You called?"

"Yes, I did Nishu."

"How is Papa?"

"Papa is improving."

"I am happy to hear that, Mom."

"I hope things are fine with you."

"Yes, Mom, everything is good."

"Good, I called you to tell that I am going shopping with Sudha and Roma tomorrow. Do you have any colour preference for reception dress?"

"Colour preference?"

"Yes, it's already a week since you flew back to Mumbai. On 15th of next month is your wedding date. I hope you remember that."

"Yes, of course I remember," I reply but truthfully, it was as if someone had woken me up from a slumber.

It was just earlier this morning that I fought with my prospective Mr Right while he was trying to explain to me how to balance personal and professional life.

I am in a catch-22 situation now, not exactly knowing how to react.

"Take care, Mom, no colour preference, you know what suits me best, I will call you tomorrow."

How could I forget about it all? That is why I told Bhai, I don't want to talk to the guy until marriage. But that idiot Preeti, deliberately goaded me to reply to his messages, so he could get to know me better. Now what do I do. I don't even have a replacement of Mr Right. Kabir came to see me and I insulted him and sent him packing. Why do I make life so complicated for myself?

I need to consider every option that fix my current situation. The only way to get my family off the back is - get a groom. Whether he is actual Mr Right, temporary Mr Right or Mr Wrong is immaterial, considering the seriousness of the situation. Other things can be managed once the bigger problem is resolved.

Not that my family has any doubts about their only daughter's potential to play tricks, but they still expected that I will at least keep to my word.

Managing the VP position seems far easier than handling my personal life, right now. I will not be able to sleep tonight for sure. Going back and talking to Samar would be like an insult and staying away from conversation would be death.

The only solution is to shamelessly message Samar early in the morning.

****

Kabir couldn't sleep either.

Nisha always rejects my efforts to repair our relationship. I never meant to do anything to hurt her.

The day she walked out of my life, was the worst day of my life. After being promoted, I had booked a sea-facing house for both of us in the heart of the city. She loves to look at the sea and I love to see her looking at it. Making her happy is all I want. I would give my life to see the two women in my life smile.

That was the time everyone in office was conspiring against her. She still doesn't know she was suspected of forging bills, which was actually orchestrated by her counterpart Kiran who left Bijals at that time. Since they were both friends, it was assumed that Nisha was equally responsible. It's only because they all feared me that nothing happened to Nisha. I never wanted to break her confidence. She wanted to work and I was just happy in her happiness.

She always misunderstood my philosophy about work. Every individual has to create one's own identity, but I didn't want Nisha to struggle as a provider. I could manage that comfortably. I have seen my mother facing so many difficulties while struggling to raise me. She should have been free to manage the house and enjoy her social work but circumstances forced her to work as a provider. Nisha would never understand that.

Kiran was using her and making corrupt deals under Nisha's name. She knew very well if Nisha was with her, she would never be blamed.

Worse was when I had to confront Mr Bijal and defend Nisha. He was quite upset and wanted her to be removed out of the system. I decided that it was time Nisha quit work and prepared for marriage. There was no need for her to struggle. She could have opened her own company and we could have happily managed our life together.

I couldn't tell her the truth—it would have only broken her. So, when she made a silly mistake I blew that petty issue out of proportion so that she would quit. As a team leader, you have to play the villain at times for the betterment of your team members.

She took the matter to heart and we actually broke up. I know the issue could have been handled in a much softer and smarter way, but unfortunately, I wasn't mature enough to handle the situation either. I do feel guilty over how I managed the issue. I want to apologise and explain the situation but she won't let me.

She was very immature back then. Though there still hasn't been much change in Nisha's temper, my love for her has increased ten-folds.

When she decided to move on from Bijals and shift to the US, the Kiran issue and her possible role in it was nearly revealed, but I intervened to resolve the matter. When the truth was finally uncovered, everyone was ashamed for the wrong allegations.

Shrija somehow managed to convince Nisha to come back. She got her back for me but I had unknowingly embedded the germ of ambition in her mind. She became determined to prove her worth and become as successful as I was.

She never realised that it was all for her. If she asked me once I would have laid down my life. All these years, I have been closely watching her grow with her hard work. Yes, hard work, the corporate shrewdness never touched my queen.

Kabir smiles, as he thinks of Nisha.

My sea-facing house is still waiting for her. I never opened that window, for I still want her to be the one to open it. The day she enters this place, it will turn into a home, our home. Her side of the cupboard is still empty, her side of bed is still empty. I want her to be by my side and not an inch away. I have never allowed anyone to sit on her chair in the dining room. My life is waiting for her to return.

****

Unaware of his side of the story, Nisha was lost, in her own life. She woke up early in the morning, followed her routine and messaged Samar in desperation.

Hey, Samar. Hope all well.

There is no response from the other side.

DP - Empty

DS –Empty

There is no status or clue to find out what Mr Right is thinking about me at this point of time.

Has he given up on me? Is he no more interested in discussing marriage? Is he hurt? Do I need to call him?

I am getting a little nervous about this situation. Controlling mood swings has become a bit difficult for me, but I am definitely not in a state to over react. Not in this situation at least, when there is no one to take the reaction. Let me just browse through the list of contacts and check people, who can come to my rescue in this troubled hour.

The situation isn't the kind I could share with anyone or ask for any help. With my past record, I know no one would support in my tricks. In many instances, the tricks had gotten people into trouble and I have shamelessly walked out of those situations taking no responsibility. But this time, is a little different, I just can't put the blame on anyone.

Kabir's number.

Ahha, it's his birthday today, he could be my saviour, let me text him on his birthday.

Happy birthday, Kabir.

Thanks, Nisha.

It was as if he was waiting for my message. After six years, he has received a message from my number, and so it becomes an important day for him.

What time should I pick you up for dinner?

Just as I wanted, another possible Mr Right against the one that I fought with yesterday morning.

All my parents want for me is marriage. I believe the guy could be their choice or mine, it doesn't matter as long as the wedding date remains the same.

My parents are very social and helpful. In time of need, anyone could approach them. They make sure they attend every social event, and feel it is a part of their social responsibility.

They feel it is important to invite all those who have invited them to their family weddings. It is a social loan and they have to pay it back.

Not having a wedding was no longer possible; it's all about the honour of Chandra family. The guy could be changed from Samar to Kabir, considering the fickle minded Chandra daughter.

Keeping this in mind, I replied immediately.

8 pm

My immediate problem sorted. There still is a potential prospect. Just before, I get ready to leave for work, I receive a message from Samar.

Hey, just read your message. Hope all well.

Oh God, why now? Why him? Can't men stick to one decision? If he was offended by yesterday's conversation, then he should maintain that. People take their own time to respond and then the whole world blames me about being impatient.

Now I would have to reply, after all it was me who

initiated this conversation. I am really not interested in looking at his DP or DS today. I could feel a sudden twist in my liking for Samar. May be it is because of this annoying behaviour or may be because of Kabir.

Hi, Samar. I'm good, how about you?

All good, so what is going on in your boring life?

Samar, don't you dare call my life boring. My life is not boring at all. It's just that to get the pulse of my kind of fun, the other person needs to be evolved enough. I am going for dinner today.

Hey, relax gorgeous. So you are going out with a bunch of friends?

No, it's my ex-boss's birthday. He has given me a special invitation.

It seems like you are in good terms with your boss.

No, not with this boss. There was a time when I was in love with him. Then we broke up and haven't gotten along since.

Why accept his invitation then?

I want to test myself. I want to see if I still have feelings for him.

Good going. All the best!

Thanks. Are you not insecure?

No, Madam, let him give it his best shot.

Why? I could fall back in love with him.

Your call. I know that you will make the right decision.

Thank you, Samar. I will catch you in the evening.

I don't know why I was honest with Samar about Kabir. I could have easily avoided telling him about dinner. Setting up a meeting with Kabir now seems like a foolish idea. Samar is quite a sensible guy. I am sure I wouldn't be risking heartache with him.

Before I could text Kabir and tell him not to come, it was 8 pm and he was at the door. Since morning, I was supposed to inform him of cancelling the date but it did not strike me.

I thought Samar would text and ask me not to go out with my ex, but he did not. Unlike most chauvinist type of guys, he does not seem to be driven by his ego. I don't know if I am pleased or upset with his gesture, either way I cannot get Samar's constant presence out of my mind.

His virtual silence is tempting me to visit his profile and see what he is up to.

DP - Cloud with silver lining

DS - All will be fine

He makes me smile.

Kabir reaches her door with a bouquet of red, pink, yellow, orange and purple roses. He wanted to take more of red but since he is colour blind, he could not make out how many red roses would give the message of his love for her that evening. There was a box of chocolates that Nisha loves. It seemed like a romantic date between two people. He rings the doorbell. She opens the door.

There stood his lady in a lovely pink satin dress, high cheekbones, silky black hair, tied from the back but left open in the front, giving her a flirty, sexy look, definitely not meant for this date, yet worn for this one. She wanted to get herself out of the stressful time spent, let down her hair and be for some entertainment, even if it was at the cost of Kabir's emotions.

Who could say that dusky, sexy, short girls don't look fabulous in pink? She almost looked like a Cinderella walking out of a fairy tale and the prince was just not prepared to handle the radiant beauty she possessed. Kabir was at a loss for words.

For Nisha, expecting any compliment from Kabir was a waste. Even if he wanted to compliment, he would not in words. She would have to read it. Nisha enjoyed reading his language of love once upon a time, but today she did not want to make that effort.

Kabir had almost lost hope that they would reconnect, he was apologetic about his past behaviour. He actually wanted to propose to Nisha.

He was ready for rejection, as he knew that one had to bear the consequences of past deeds. Nisha was all set to take the revenge, she could feel those vibes from him, but this time it was her chance to teach him a lesson long- pending.

He apologised for the day before, she smiled, but did not forgive, they talked, they laughed, they enjoyed and they had a good time. Nisha was reminded of the time they spent together.

As they walked along the passage to the dining hall of a lavish five-star hotel, she saw a couple walking just ahead of them. This seemed to be their first date. Interesting was the height gap between the couple, it was exactly the same as Nisha and Kabir.

She felt as if they were a set of their clones walking ahead. The girl seemed to be in her late teens while the guy in his late twenties. It was an awkward gap but what Nisha could connect was the anxiety of going for a first date, which clearly was visible from the girl's behaviour. He gently tried to touch her hand but the girl would not allow, he tried to walk along with her but in haste she would step out. He would try to make her feel comfortable and in turn she would become more uncomfortable.

Nisha was watching it all mischievously as Kabir was lost in the happiness of the moment. She turned to Kabir to comment about the situation and found him looking at her.

"Kabir don't try that with me, or you will receive a painful reminder of how hard I can punch."

The statement was enough to get Kabir back from wonderland and accept reality. But he still maintained his intentions of the dinner very clear. He did propose to her, but she did not reject nor did she accept. Neither did she tell him the truth. She no longer felt the need for revenge. She felt it was a perfect fresh start. She did not even feel the need to say a word.

After the dinner and a long drive, they sat by the sea. Nisha loved that spot. She was so happy sitting there after a very long time. Work made her forget most of the things she enjoyed doing. Her first love was to sit next to the sea for hours. Being from Nagpur, she never got a chance to see what it is to be on the land that ends towards the sea. She wanted to make the most of the evening and so did Kabir. He just wanted to see her do all she loved.

She wanted to have an ice cream before he drove her home. It was their usual custom to have a goodnight ice cream before dropping her off. Forgetting that they were no more together he brought just one cup that was ritually to be shared by both of them. He looked happy. Nisha understood but she reminded him to get another cup for himself. He smiled to himself and pretended that he is not in a mood, while hiding his spoon. She ate her cup without even asking him to share. Kabir kept looking at her.

After a lovely time, Kabir dropped her home. For him it was nice to see a changed Nisha, it was after six years that they had spent time together. Kabir did not want to make any wrong move to spoil the evening. It was important for him to drop her back in a happy mood. Nisha was a girl who never allowed him to gift her anything, she always paid for her share of food and fun. She wanted to be equal and fair in their relationship. She never allowed her boyfriend to pamper her. It was unusual but it was a fact. In the office, she was his junior and she wanted to maintain a decorum even in real life. She never understood how to play two different roles with the same person in one life.

Kabir was, however, very practical and knew how to balance both the things well. He would be professional in office and a mad lover outside. Bijal's was not a place where a couple could not work together. Mr Bijal's daughter looked after the finance and his son-in-law looked after exports.

****

It was a lovely evening. I am so happy.

"Yes, I love him and will keep loving him till the end of my life."

But yes guilty for Samar at the same time, he must have messaged me. I quickly check the phone. But there is no message.

DP - Lots of smiling children

DS - Trust her more than life.

I feel even guiltier now. I have no intention of ditching him, but I am not sure of my own mind.

Hi Samar.

No reply from him for over an hour is making me feel bad. I am not able to sleep. I send one more message.

Hello, where are you, Mr Samar?

:-) – Aaha! to my relief he replies.

Why are you smiling Samar?

Hey, gorgeous how was the evening?

Gorgeous? Have you seen me?

Of course, I have.

Hmm…

It seems like you had a fight with your ex-boyfriend/ boss.

No, not really.

So then how come you remembered me?

If you can believe me—I was missing you.

That is why you wore that lovely pink dress?

Pink! Samar did you see me?

No, just guessing. I was just imagining how beautiful you look. The beauty of a woman lies in her eyes.

You think so?

Yes, I believe in it. Did he propose to you?

Yes, he did.

And you are now in four minds.

Meaning?

You know what I mean, my princess. You are too funny.

I know. But I am not a princess. Please keep it to Ms Nisha. It feels better that way.

How can you be so candid about what you are?

Meaning?

You should keep a few things to yourself or else things might lead you into trouble.

Till today being honest has worked in my favour.

I like that.

Trust me, I can't be what I am not.

Good to know that, Ms. Nisha. So you have two options in hand now.

For?

For marriage.

I always had enough options in hand for marriage, Mr Samar.

Don't get offended, Ms Nisha.

I am just telling you the tragic achievement of my life. I have always had ample options available.

Let's not get into another fight, Ms Nisha. We don't have much time in hand. Your mother called my mom to go shopping.

And what did you say?

Nothing, I thought of informing Aunty that her daughter has called the marriage off.

Then did you tell her?

No, I thought, let us take another chance. There are still 21 days in hand. And I am quite a charmer. You may call me a *Baazigar*.

What?

Relax, my princess. Would you mind if I say that even I love Hindi Cinema?

Of course not. Why would I?

So Madam, *Haar kar jitne waale ko baazigar kehete* **hain.**

Very filmy.

Very, very real, Madam.

Feeling a bit relaxed now. Thank God, all is well.

Goodnight. Will catch you later. I have to wake up early for a meeting tomorrow.

Yes, things are improving. If you are honest, you don't have to play tricks. I am still not very confident about the way things are happening, but am prepared to take them as they come. I have not yet shared the news of my wedding with anyone in the office. It isn't even a month since I have been promoted, sharing such news might get many eyebrows raised and opportunists will get a chance to undermine my position. I need to play safe as much as possible.

Next day, I get a surprise. The MD, Mr Bijal informs me that in four days I have to go for a vendor visit to China. The company wants to bring some Chinese technology to India, and needs someone to go there and understand its viability for an Indian business house and its feasibility in terms of Indian conditions. Being technically involved in the project, I was the best person to go. The trip is ten day long, which means I would be back just six days before the D-Day.

She needed this break even if it was a work trip. Not that life was difficult, but she needed time, time to think, time to ponder upon and time to prepare for a

lifelong commitment. Lifelong decisions are not made with short-term tricks.

What if Samar acted extra smart? What if he refuses to allow me to take care of my parents after marriage? He needs to be conditioned enough to let me live my life. As of now, he seems to be responsive and understanding but that might be a temporary pretence.

There have been so many stories of people completely changing their colours after marriage and I am scared of them. The sole reason for me to agree to this alliance is papa. I could survive Kabir, who had one personality at work and another outside work. His duality confused me. I am not sure if I can deal with another one like him.

By now I know that the two worlds are completely different. When it comes to work you only need basic training and certain level of behavioural skill set, coupled with presence of mind, but personal life is very complex. Every step of it has to be carefully planned. And no plan actually works.

It only survives on the principles of love, trust and sacrifice. There are always tactful conditions applied when you are at work, while your personal life is unconditional giving. I could now relate things to Kabir's behaviour.

Shrija always says I only know half the truth, may be, but still I could never understand the reason for Kabir's obnoxious behaviour that led us to our break-up.

I have never been happy after leaving him. A part of my life was paralysed. No matter how much I pretend the evening made me fall back in love with Kabir.

I wanted him to hold my hand and walk along, wanted him to share the ice cream and give me a goodnight kiss. This exactly is the reason I always avoid him. I still love him and I know that very well!

****

With only four days to leave for China, I had a lot to do. Most importantly informing my mother. I need to inform her in such a way that she doesn't think I am running away from the situation. I just don't want her to misquote me in front of bhai.

Chapter 13

Nisha is excited as this is her first trip to China. She had been to Singapore and Australia in the past. She knew she would not be connected with Samar for over a week. A ten-day gap would hopefully help her unwind and think about life from a fresh perspective. One of the main reasons she agreed to this trip. She picks up her phone to inform Samar, instead gets a message from him.

Hey, Princess, did I scare you?

No why?

You are running away from me for ten days. It's not even fifteen days since we started talking and you already decided to take a break.

Oh, Samar I was just about to tell you. Mom must have told you.

No.

Then how do you know?

My mom told me.

I am sure my mother must have informed her. But I was just about to tell you about this sudden business trip. There is nothing to hide, trust me and I am not running from you.

Hmmm…

I am strong enough to face the situation.

Don't get stressed. I trust you completely, Madam.

Neither can I leave this story abruptly in between nor would Samar let me do that. Above all this, Samar has the support of Suraj bhai, my hard-hearted devil brother. Somewhere I feel it is the fear of my brother that is influencing my behaviour.

Samar understands, he will not misunderstand the situation. He will not jump into unnecessary conclusions, just like bhai.

Yes, he is quite calculative in his approach, yet reasonable at the same time. Mostly guys love to blame the girl either for being a snob or non-cooperative. He is proving himself different from the league.

Thanks, Samar. – I reply

What is your favourite flower?

What? Why?

Just want to send you a bouquet of flowers. Only if you are fine with it, of course.

Where in Mumbai do you stay?

Bandra.

Really? That is really interesting.

Why? Do you want me to send my location via Google Maps?

No ☺

Flower?

Roses and lots of them ☺.

Life is becoming more romantic with each passing day and I am enjoying every bit of it. I visit Samar's profile as usual.

DP – Lots of roses. All colours.

DS - All for you.

I copy his DP and DS, just for some fun and send it back to him with a wink. He smiles back.

Kabir is in office and I think he will call me to talk about last evening. I am sure that he is hurt by my rude behaviour.

I receive a call, but that is from the reception about an evening event. There is a small farewell party organised for one of the oldest employees at Bijals. He is moving to Australia to settle down with his son. Mr. Brahma Kukreja, his name means 'God of creation' and so is his contribution in building Bijals.

A jolly good man who makes everyone smile. He helped me learn about the organisation when I was new to the work culture. Where Kabir introduced work to me, Brahma Sir helped me understand the work culture. He was a part of my life for eight years, though in my second inning with the company his role reduced. I will always be thankful to him.

I am probably the last one to reach at the office party hall, Maria had to call to remind me the party. Last minute work always takes time.

Let me walk fast else everything will be over by the time I reach.

As I step towards the party hall, I see the entire passage has a different view, it is full of roses—and lots of them. Different colours and different sizes. I just love this sight, they remind me of the lovely bouquet Kabir brought last night and on a second thought of Samar, who just gave a hint of sending flowers across to me.

I clicked a lot of pictures, in excitement. Whoever had made this arrangement has done a fabulous job. I reach the party hall just when the event was about to conclude.

Mr Brahma was standing in front of a lovely backdrop full of roses, giving his farewell speech. It was a very touching moment for all of us. He stood as a strong pillar with Mr Bijal all through his work journey.

This is not the first time, that our office has been decorated to celebrate a send-off, but never before had roses struck me so much.

I laughed at myself, at my foolishness.

Nisha, you are mad, you think Samar could have arranged this decoration for you. Why are you so hopelessly silly? Why do you let your imaginations run wild?

I better get off this fanciful dream and meet Mr Brahma, or I will give into the temptation to call Samar.

It's just too late now. Karishma will yell at me, when I reach home. I promised her a dinner outing today.

Even while driving home, I was smiling continuously.

The lights of my residence basement, are brighter than usual, may be someone has a party at home. Just a quick glance around and hello! There are so many roses here. Am I in some dreamland? I pinch myself! But nothing could get me sane, there are roses all over. I am so sure it's Samar. I was right, he did decorate my place with roses.

Let me message him, but before I could type, my phone beeps. It's him again!

Hey Princess, hope you like the décor.

Samar, are you a florist? – I feel it's better to check before reality gives me a shocker that I am married to a 'foolwalaa'

Anything for you, Ma'am.

Samar, I'm confused. Did you get my office décor done?

Office? No, I can't even dare to disturb your workspace, but after we get married, I can. Right?

Right.

I am still confused, may be the décor is done by the same vendor and that's why it looks so similar. Take a chill pill Nisha, *'bade bade sheheroon mein choti choti baatein hote reheti hain'.*

Do you like it Nisha?

I just love it, Samar. Your taste is amazing.

Anything for you. Did you enter the house?

Hey just entering, are you able to see me?

There is a camera inside your mobile, which connects you to me directly.

Samar, be serious. I understand technology very well. How do you know where I am?

Ms Technology, what is so difficult in understanding how I am tracing you? If I can get all of this done then I can very well know where you are. Right?

God I am so confused. If you allow me, can I enter my house?

Please Princess.

Interior of my house is decorated so well. Wow! There is box of chocolate and a lovely pink dress. I am being pampered. My God, how did he manage to get in? Did Karishma know about my marriage? I did not tell her. Samar will get me killed. It's not really nice to be manipulative with your own people. You don't need to strategize against them, they will be happy in your happiness. But hello, I never gave him permission to buy me anything. We are not married yet.

Did you speak to Karishma? – I immediately message.

Are you scared of her?

No. but she knows I don't accept gifts from anyone.

So in that case Princess, I told her that it's all from her husband, who apparently is my friend too.

You are just too much, Samar. Why will her husband gift me?

Because there is something interesting that you will know very soon.

Really! What are you up to Samar?

I am just trying to impress you and you are not even co-operating. You don't want to know about me. You don't

want to talk to me. You have put so many restrictions on yourself and me. You have not yet disclosed about our marriage to anyone. I am not even sure whether you want to marry me or not.

This message comes to me as a shocker, never realised that I am playing with someone's emotions.

I am sorry, Samar. Give me some time, shall sort it out. Thanks for being so understanding. – Immediately I reply.

Strange there is someone who is subtly making me realise that I am wrong – for the first time in my life I admit – yes this time I am.

Good night, Ms Nisha, you must be tired, let's connect tomorrow.

Thanks, goodnight.

****

Next three days were quite hectic, she had to complete as much work as possible. After returning from China she would not have enough time to close pending work. She finalised the new house where she would be shifting to, after her return. Karishma also had something to share with her. She had decided to move back with her husband.

It looked like Samar played an important role here. Nisha still did not want to know who Samar was or how he was connected to Karishma's husband but as long as her friend was happy, Nisha was happy.

Nisha was also developing feelings for Samar. Whatever he said or did had a meaning. She might find it stupid in the beginning but with time, she would realise a logical and sensible reason behind it. She was nearly convinced that she should marry him, to the point that she was making serious efforts to detach herself from the charm of Kabir.

It was as if forcing herself away from the magnet. She thought the China trip would be a breather for her.

Kabir was trying hard to win her back, but Nisha was deliberately reminding herself of what he did to her, six years back. Suraj had almost stopped talking to her. Roma was in constant touch. There was a jigsaw of emotions, but as they say everything happens for a reason.

Escaping from it all, Nisha boarded her flight to China. The flight was really long and she was grateful that the company arranged for a car and a driver to take her around, when she landed.

Nisha had interacted with Mr. Paul many times, since her first year at Bijal, as the company had tie-ups with the Chinese Company since the very first year. The head of the Chinese company and the director of Bijal were friends. They wanted to bring Chinese technology to India.

Mr Paul was in charge of technology development and spent a lot of time, guiding her and explaining how each piece of technology worked and who was the potential user, whenever she had to pitch the concept to her sales team in India. Though they never met in person but their understanding was brilliant.

Nisha's trip to China was to examine a new piece of technology. Her goal was to spend time with Mr. Paul and get a firm understanding of the product. Unfortunately, the trip wasn't well planned. Mr. Paul was on leave during her first two days in China. Instead of wasting those two days, Nisha set up a meeting with members of his department, which, not only helped her gain an understanding of the technology and fill in the gaps in her research, it also ensured that she was able to ask sensible questions to Mr. Paul once they meet.

On landing, she was driven directly to the office and she spent the day understanding the basic structure of the technology. The next day was dedicated to site visit - viewing the working model and getting a hands-on experience.

The first day was pretty long, even though there wasn't too much of a time difference. She was dead tired, when she finally arrived at her room. She wasn't looking forward to another day of work, especially not the 150 km drive to view the working model. Just as she was unwinding for the day, to her frustration, her cell phone beeped.

Hi, Ms Nisha. Hope you reached safe.

I have no energy, but reply 'yes' because the messenger is my-should-be husband.

Just need a quick answer.

Tell me.

What is your favourite colour?

What?

Mom is going shopping tomorrow, she wants to know.

Brown.

I reply and switch off before the cell beeps again.

Feeling really frustrated, I like him, but just don't enjoy his claim over my time. This is 'why' I did not want to interact with him.

Why am I even reacting to his silly questions? I don't even know whether he is Mr Right. Moreover, I don't even know him well enough to share my favourite things.

The next day I wake up two hours late.

Never in my life have I been even a single minute late for work and today......I am two hours late...!

I quickly get ready. As I enter the office, I apologise every single person I meet. Time is worshipped in this company and nobody dares to disrespect it. Thankfully, no one is offended as I am a guest and the person I am supposed to meet is not around.

I start talking to junior executives to understand the technology. Their technology seems very logical, usually when people fill their tanks through the motor machine, they don't bother to switch it off until water starts overflowing. The water tank, the company was producing uses sensor technology that sounded an alarm to inform the filler that the desired volume of water has been reached. If it was a 300-litre tank, an alarm would sound at once 150 litres is filled, then when

225 litres and finally when the water level reaches 290 litres. These alarms enable the filler to stop the filling process once water reaches desired level. Moreover, for convenience at each stage the alarm had a different music. This adaptation is useful not only in saving electricity, but also preventing water from being wasted. Once the mechanism was explained, we took on a tour of the actual working model. The company wants to launch these tanks in India soon, since it seems to be a sunrise industry.

Once the tour was over, we went to the best place in town for lunch. I became friends with an Indian from the team of technicians. This girl is four or five years younger and graduated from the same engineering college as mine. She must have been in her first year, when I was in my final year or may be joined after I finished college. We spoke about our college days, the great places to eat and famous nearby hangouts. Overall, the lunch was a relaxing experience. After lunch, I got the required information, resolved all the concerns and returned to the hotel.

I finally relaxed. Meeting my junior was like walking down the memory lane. It was in college that I started on my journey to build an identity - from being the most pampered and overprotected only girl child of the family to becoming who I am today.

I could see her as my reflection, but with a lot of difference. Sheena is married and settled in this town with her husband. Both of them work for the same company, their baby is too small to go to school, so is taken care of by his grandparents. Life was simple and set for her.

Why can't it be as simple and set for me? What does she possess that I don't? Why does her contentment leave me restless? Why is she so settled - in her mind and accepting of everything around? Why am I so different from her?

I feel there is something seriously wrong with me, either I have too high expectations or I am taking life a little too seriously.

I think I am lucky, to have Samar, and yes, I am even luckier to have been able to teach Kabir a lesson. Do I still love Kabir? Yes, he was once the love of my life. He always says that I don't understand him but the fact is that he never understood me. Our relationship was suffocated by misunderstandings. I need to resolve my feelings. I need to make one of the most crucial decision of my life. I need to make this decision now. I will be getting married in just over two weeks and I haven't even informed anyone in the office. It clearly shows how unsettled I am with my priorities. By the time I am back in India, there won't be much time left for the wedding. I have to apply for at least a month of leave. I haven't discussed or made any plans with Samar. I don't even know if he will be open to me working or if we will be living in Mumbai. At this level, people hardly leave their careers; how do I know for sure that he will let me decide?

What if he doesn't? What if his mother says her daughter-in-law shouldn't work? Will he make me sit at home? After all, he is only getting married to me because his mother smiled after hearing my name. What a funny reason it is, to marry someone, but of course less funny than mine.

Oh! His message again, this guy will live long. Every

time I think of him, he is there, to be honest I keep thinking about him.

Mom bought this sari for you, is it fine? - He sends me a pic.

Yes.

Have you seen it, Nisha?

Yes.

I don't want to get into a long conversation with him. I want to avoid any kind of difference of opinion. I want that our opinions should match.

I know I am compromising at every step with Samar. I am trying to understand him, but I have never tried to understand Kabir. I never gave him a chance to put across his point of view. I have always been so reactive with Kabir but with Samar, I am developing patience, evolving as a person. It is a big change.

****

Now I am tired of this unplanned trip. Mr Bijal is known for his sudden decisions, which get his work done for sure, but at the cost of other people's comfort. He is very superstitious; he believes in numbers. Some pandit told him that if he starts anything on his birth date or with his birth number or worked with people whose birth numbers matches his, then his business would grow fast. He always does that. Right from the first day when he decided to float this company and surprisingly, this number game worked for him, and his company grew leaps and bounds.

The first fresher to have the same date of birth as his, was me, as an experiment he hired me and after that it so happened that mostly people with the similar status started becoming a part of the company. Kabir is one of the few exceptions. He always challenges his numerology belief and often proves it wrong. Somewhere Mr.Bijal is scared of him and in heart of hearts wants to be defeated by him. I know he himself is going through an inner conflict.

This sudden trip was not need of the hour, but it so happened that astrologically, Mr Bijal's stars favoured the deal only during this period, and so, he had to send someone, who understood the technology thoroughly, hence me.

Thankfully this trip had no connection with my numerology. I was sent as a useful, value adding resource. Times have changed for me now.

Sometimes, situations are not in your control nor do you want them to be in control.

I never believed in this number theory, but my decisions are still not as simple as Mr Bijals. If I marry Kabir, life would not be as complicated, as it would be with Samar, after all he has learnt his lesson and he already knows me and my priorities. I have worked with him and we could be good life partners. If I marry Samar, nothing would be certain, as he only exists as a virtual person in my life. I could continue whatsapp conversation with him all my life, without knowing him, seeing him, hearing him or meeting him.

I have to decide fast. No counselling would help me. It's going to be purely my heart that would have to decide for me.

Back home, her parents were waiting for her to arrive and here, she was fighting a battle within herself. If she shared this complication with anyone it would seem stupid.

Yes, people think that I take too much of stress about things that can be taken easy, but it is hard to understand why such an important decision is not given sufficient thought by most people.

May be marriage as an institution is made only to discipline a man-woman relationship. That is why it is so easy for people to declare it socially, without even knowing if they will be able to live up-to that social acceptance. I fear social acceptance more than others. People take it too lightly.

I always wanted to prepare myself to be able to accept my relationship personally first and then declare it socially. I have seen too many people getting married and then not honouring their marriage like Rahul, Shaina and Natasha.

Rahul is married but still has an affair every six months. I would kill such a man, if he ever comes my way. Shaina is having an extramarital affair with her boss. I'd rather remain single than be less than fully committed to my husband and cheat on him behind his back. Natasha decided to get married but she spends all her time cribbing about her husband and her in-laws. I would either accept them with open arms with all their positives and negatives, than taking a step ahead and regretting. After all, nobody is perfect, especially not me.

I want to take these decisions, but before that, I have to be sure of how and where the life would head. There has to be fun, there has to be togetherness and commitment in this adventurous, unpredictable journey.

My cell did not beep and so I was quite relaxed. Yet I am scared, what if it beeps?

The next day started pretty early. She was ready before time, her cab was waiting for her, and she reached office half an hour early. People smiled at her, thinking about the chaos she created the day before, many were not present to see her, but were informed about it by other colleagues. The Indian guest is very funny.

The receptionist asked her to be seated in the waiting area, as Mr. Paul, the VP of technology was to arrive in following 15 minutes. This meeting was a great honour for her, as Mr. Paul had been there to answer her technical queries and guide her as she learnt her role as Senior Project Manager and now, VP of technology. The interaction was mostly through mails, phone calls, messages and video conferences; she was finally going to meet the man face to face.

Mr. Paul goes to greet her at the reception the moment he arrives. He too was glad to finally meet her. He greets her warmly and asks her to wait for another fifteen minutes so he could settle himself.

The meeting goes extremely fruitful for both of

them. The exchange of knowledge takes place at equal wavelength. He gave her insights on the technology. They spoke about lots of things. He being an intelligent man knows every minute detail of the business and Nisha being a sharp technical person grasps each and every detail shared.

He shares with her a very basic rule of this game.

"Nisha, there is nothing extraordinary about this technology, what makes it popular is the simple feature that solves everyday problem for people. You don't have to be intelligent; you have to be a consumer to understand what he wants. As technical people, we are blessed to create such things, just like how a doctor knows which medicine would work on this machine called body; likewise we technicians should know which technique would make life easier for the users."

I like the way he explains, sometimes you complicate things for no reason, but usually a simple problem is overrated only so that the solution can be overcharged. You do business out of a reason to exist.

On the last day of my trip, Mr. Paul invites me to his home for dinner. His wife is a very warm person, an Indian by origin who enjoys having a piece of home with Indian visitors.

The two of them had met in India at her father's restaurant, when he visited some 25 years back. Mr Paul got smitten while she resolved a customer query. He came up to her and said that he liked her honesty. During his one month stay in India, he dined at her restaurant every night. At the end of his trip, he realised that he was in love with her and wanted to marry her. Her father wasn't pleased but despite the opposition, she accepted his proposal, they got married and she shifted to China. They have a happy life with two pretty girls both in college now.

Mr Paul and his wife, Shruti, promise to visit me on their next trip to India. I hope to give them the same warm welcome when they come home. Looking at them, it feels that marriages are made in heaven, it is not as difficult as it seem to me. They are people from two different countries living together in such a beautiful relation.

****

Next morning I fly back and I am glad I applied for a day's leave to relax and unwind.

I made sure that all the reports and mails were sent to the concerned, so that they were updated about my learning. Mr.Paul was right there is nothing complicated about the technology, nor is there any need to have a Joint-Venture with this Chinese company, we can surely make in India. Post sending my reports I wanted to be free to relax for a day.

The moment she reached home, she called her parents.

"Mom, I am back," I said sing out at the top of my voice.

Mom was puzzled for a while, as I wasn't in Nagpur, but Mumbai. She relaxed once she realised that at least I am in India and soon would be with them.

I know all she want is happiness for her only daughter, her mad daughter.

I call Kabir to inform him that I am back. He too reciprocated with the same warmth. The vibes were good, but during the whole course of the day, I did not see the message that was lying in my inbox.

Evening I read the message from Samar —

Welcome home, Ms Nisha.

The message makes me neither happy nor sad; rather it makes me think—if I should dump him and ask Kabir if he would marry me. After all, I don't even know Samar. If it is about commitment then Samar and I have known each other only for past 3 weeks, while Kabir has been committed to me for last 8 years. So what if we broke up in between! Yes, during this time, Kabir might have looked at other girls as prospective wives but even I met other men as potential husbands. Fate decided that neither of us would find the right person, so, maybe we are destined for each other. And when two people are made for each other than where is the need for a third person?

Kabir asks me out for a lunch date and without a second thought I agree.

"Am I sure about him?" I ask myself just before leaving. Then answer my own question, not clear about him, but about the decision of getting settled — yes, I am sure about myself.

Stop doubting your decisions Nisha. If he fits into the criteria then well and good else - move on. I will tell him everything and not hide anything from him; as it is honesty makes things simple.

With this thought, she gets ready for lunch.

Kabir comes exactly on time and she goes with him to their favourite place where they used to eat during their initial days with less money, not because he had less money but because he wanted to reminisce the old days.

She opens the conversation with few, simple words.

"Kabir, I got my promotion letter before leaving for China."

"Yes, I know, so what is the next plan?"

"I plan on getting married now," I say and the water glass fell from Kabir's hands.

"Married?"

A waiter comes to the rescue trying to clean the table, but Kabir asks him to leave while keeping his eyes firmly on me. I don't know what he was up to. I did not say anything wrong.

"Yes, married, Kabir. I was always supposed to get married, as you very well know."

"So was I," he replies.

"I never stopped you."

"Nor did I stop you," he says getting irritated.

"So now I am getting married." Now I was finding this conversation stupid. I had come to discuss something else with him and we are taking our discussion to another tangent altogether.

"Wish you a happy married life, Nisha. Is this why you came out with me? You wanted to tell me now that you have come to my level, you are choosing to marry another man. What is the goal? To make me realise what a chauvinist pig I have been? Oh please, Nisha, of all the women at least you don't have to behave like a melodramatic queen. I never did anything wrong to you. Have you ever noticed yourself? You are so engrossed in yourself that you don't even realise the other person's presence in your life.

Do you think when your aim was to become what you are today; you would have ever been able to live a normal, married life. You always took my achievements as new challenges to beat. You never took me as a man in your life, you considered me a benchmark and as your competition." He went on and on and on…

"I never did that, Kabir."

"You did that, you were always like this, you could never understand that in a relationship there are two people, a man whose job is to provide everything to make his wife and their kids happy and the other one is a woman whose job is to make the whole family happy with whatever he provides. You thought that you are a man. You were always competing not only against me but also yourself."

"I was not, Kabir. In a relationship there is a thing called respect, and that was always missing from your side. Whenever I wanted to tell you that I could do this you always insulted me, discouraged me, you wanted me to feel less about myself. Why? Am I not a human?"

"You are a woman who has to know her gifts; there is no need to keep proving yourself in the man's world. Your job is to make the world beautiful. You are gifted with a creative mind, use that, there is no need to fight this man's world."

"Kabir, you are impossible. I didn't come here to discuss this."

"Oh, OK, so did you come here to give me your wedding invitation and show me your appraisal letter?"

"Oh please, Kabir, grow up. I did not come here to discuss my professional life, but talk to you about our personal life. Something that you thought was missing in my conversations with you. It was my mistake to have accepted your invitation. Though at least now I know for sure I am taking the right decision. See you in the office, counterpart."

I leave the table, nothing has changed between us and it's still the same. The fights have not changed, only years have gone by. We are both now almost 10 years older from where we started, he is no more my senior, yet I have to prove my worth at every stage.

Today I just don't care for him. I don't care about anything in the world. I can't take a wrong decision.

She cries for hours after reaching home.

Thank god I did not tell Kabir the actual reason for meeting him, thank god I did not tell him that I wanted to marry him and nobody else. I am hurt by his behaviour, he has still not changed. How can someone never understand your feelings despite knowing you so well?

But it is good to have known that he still has not changed and he never will. I don't know why I thought that he must have. How could I be so wrong about him?

I thought that, since we are still single and there was no one else in our lives ever since we parted, we were meant to be together. Instead of thinking of spending one full life with an unknown person, it was better to live it happily with the person whom you have known for so long. What was wrong with my logic?

I thought with my heart, not my mind. Thank God, I have someone sensible in my life. Suraj Bhai was right! I should have trusted him blindly. After all, he is my brother and knows what is right for me. He is a far better judge of character than myself.

She thinks enough to get back to conversation with Samar.

Hi Samar, I am finally back to action.

She sees a message from Suraj asking her when she was flying to Nagpur. She decides to go back home as soon as possible.

She decides to shift to the company house within next three days. All arrangements were to be done for her parents well before time. Parent's room, kitchen, *puja* room, dining room, sitting balcony, walking area, maid, paper man, milkman. Everything. Thankfully, the new house was close by so she did not have to spend too much time and energy on these jobs.

She also mailed her boss to ask for leave.

Dear Sir,

This is to inform that due to some unavoidable circumstances, I need two weeks leave from work. I understand that as a senior with responsibilities, it is important for me to prove myself worthy of the promotion, but before taking charge I need to sort out a few personal matters.

Thanks and regards,
Nisha.

She thought that she would get the reply next day morning, but to her surprise she receives an immediate reply.

Dear Nisha,

Is everything fine? Tell me what is the matter? You have never taken two weeks off in your entire career with us.

Regards,
Bijal

Dear Sir,

I have decided to get married.

Regards,

Nisha

Dear Nisha,

Leave granted. Where is our invitation card?

Regards,
Bijal

She sent back a smile as she had no card to give. She thought it would be a private affair and she would not be inviting anyone from office. Her MD knew her very well, for she was like a daughter who had grown up in the last eight years and now was starting a new life. He wished the best for her.

Nisha smile to herself.

I must be the funniest bride on earth. I don't even know whom I am marrying.

Nisha decides to meet her friends at a coffee shop and invite them for the wedding. She thanked God for coffee shops, they create an environment, where people can feel good, relax and rejuvenate. These shops are like heaven for people under stress. Who says you need liquor or drugs to relieve tension, a cup of coffee is enough.

They were there till 1:30 am, even Karishma joined her gang of friends. Nisha had avoided looking at the cell phone, as she did not want anyone to know the background. When asked about the guy, she just smiled and asked them to come and meet him personally at the wedding. The moment she reached home, first thing she saw was her cell phone and yes, there was a message for her.

Are you fine?

DP - Moon

DS - Good night

Yes.

You are awake till so late? What happened? I messaged quite some time back.

Nothing, I went out with friends.

OK, goodnight, now sleep.

****

I find this behaviour very irritating. What is the point in such a conversation, where I am treated like a little girl? But then, how can I forget the big fight that I had in the afternoon, where I got a man to treat me as equal. I feel like calling Samar to check if he thinks of me in the same way, will he give me space. I feel like calling it off with Samar because I don't know if he would be able to understand me. Just as Kabir failed, Samar too could fail. I don't want the same story to repeat, it is better to be single than being heartbroken.

The whole point of not wanting to know Samar, was simple. If I am not able to judge points that would lead to compatibility, then I would equally not judge him for points on incompatibility and same goes with him.

I better not complicate things and make an attempt to go with the flow. Papa is more important than anyone else in the world. If I have to compromise with Samar for papa's happiness then I will. But at least I need to inform him about the lunch meeting with Kabir, after all he should know about it.

Mr Samar, just wanted to inform that I met Kabir for lunch today and had a fight with him.

You meet people for lunch to fight?

Oh God, Mr Samar why are you so difficult?

Goodnight, Ms Nisha, you don't have to get bothered about such things. You are an independent person and you can meet anyone you want.

Will you be fine if I work even if we get married?

It's your choice, Ms Nisha, as long as you are happy you can do anything.

Are you just pretending to be good? I sometimes feel that you are just too good to be true.

I am who I am. I can't behave any differently. Why do I need to pretend in front of you?

You, Mr Samar, are too difficult to understand. Instead of getting into an argument with you, I think I will sleep, I do have work tomorrow. Let us chat with a fresh mind in the morning. Goodnight :)

Better. Goodnight.

Conversations with him always cause mental chaos. He was so different from all the guys I know. Is he pretending to be nice or is he genuinely that nice? I am not a daughter of some millionaire who he has to marry to eliminate his debts. I cannot figure this man out. I actually like him but I am still caught in a dilemma. God, why don't you make my life a little simple?

****

Next day as she enters office she starts receiving words of congratulations from colleagues.

"So finally someone has agreed to tie the knot"

"Lucky year dear, first promotion, then China trip, a new house and now marriage, was it all planned?"

"Tell us about the guy, do we know him?"

Nisha did not know how to react. She wasn't prepared to answer these kinds of questions to her colleagues. This matter was supposed to be kept under wraps in office. How was she supposed to tell anyone that even she didn't know him?

Nisha wanted to leave this entire public spectacle, pack her bags and go home. She needed peace for herself. She was going to start a new life, a life where she could no longer take any decision independently. Every choice would be dependent on the choices of a stranger, her new life partner. She smiled at everyone and informed them, the date and venue, invited them, though deep inside she did not want anyone to come.

One person was watching all this with no admiration. He had seen a different person a day before. He had seen the devil of a woman who would kill if asked questions that she didn't like, but today she was not responding at all. He kept on looking at her silently, for he knew he had no role to play.

She passed him as she walked to her boss's cabin.

"Sir, good morning"

"Good morning, my girl. So now you are a grown- up girl who's getting married."

"Please, Sir, I am not going anywhere, it's just that instead of staying with Karishma, I will be officially staying with a man, a husband. Nothing else will change in life."

"You are definitely not going anywhere. Do you think I would ever let you go anywhere? But you are wrong, getting married changes everything. You will have to change your perspective towards life. Everything has to have an 'us' factor in it and not 'I' factor. You have lived enough for yourself, now live for your husband and later, your children."

She keeps silent and asks for permission to leave.

He gives her permission and as she walks to her cabin, she could almost hear violins playing in the background as if to bid her farewell. She tries to keep her face emotionless. She didn't want to give into her fears. She didn't want to face Mr Right, a seemingly nice guy who she has never met. She wanted to give her Mr Right a face, she wanted it to be Kabir but after that chaos, she knew it couldn't be him.

She tries to distract herself, by listing down all the things that were to be completed before she left for Nagpur. It was a huge list and two weeks is a long time for a workaholic like her. The Ex VP Technical was asked to continue till she returned back.

Kabir was dumped in a corner of her mind, but Samar was never given a thought.

It was a strange situation she was in. She thinks of her friend, a Bihari, who shaved her head just because India lost a match. She was a loner and enjoyed her life to the core, but now she was married, happy with

her husband and a cute child, Vihaan. Nisha used to appreciate her for her bold decisions, but could never understand what caused her 360 degree change, from a wild wanderer to a willing wife.

She calms herself by thinking of the hundreds of people who are happily married. She thinks about her mother, the happiest woman on earth, who loves her husband and wants her daughter to reach the next stage of her life.

Chapter 14

Mumbai Airport

As I stand at the airport waiting to board the plane to my new life, I notice Mr Wrong.

What is Kabir doing here?

Should I speak to him? Should I ignore him?

We have been fighting for years over promotions and conflicting egos. Should I make peace before I start my new life? Get him out of my mind, my heart and my life?

Before I could make up my mind, he approaches me. "Hi, Nisha, travelling home?"

"Yes, I'm going home. Don't pretend like you didn't know."

"When are you coming back?"

"Excuse me? That is none of your business. You are not my boss. Kabir I don't want to argue with you anymore. Just leave me alone. I am going home to get married."

"OK, all the best in life. I'm sure the man you are marrying is a very lucky guy."

"Shut up, Kabir."

"Nisha, you are overreacting. What have I done wrong? I only offered you best wishes. How is that wrong now?"

"I know what you really mean."

"Nisha, I meant what I said. Why do you always assume the worst? You are the one who walked into my life and you are the one who walked out. You fought and proved all you wanted. I never really had a role to play because you didn't let me."

Why is he doing this? I am finally moving forward and he is once again barging in making an attempt to ruin everything. I will not let him do that anymore.

"Kabir, please go and let me be happy. I am going to make a new start and it can't begin with a fight with you."

I walk away, pull out my phone, hoping a quick chat with Samar to get rid of my irritation. There is a message from him and I am once again reassured that he is my Mr Right.

Reached the airport?

Yes, reached the airport, Samar. Thanks for your concern. When are you coming?

Tonight.

OK.

I wanted to talk to him more, but I was afraid my mood would affect this conversation. He has been very patient with me all through all of my doubts. He has never made me feel stupid about myself. I truly feel like I know him even without meeting him. I am sure my marriage to him will be a happy one.

Take care, Nisha. Don't get too worked up about things. Everything will be fine. I know you and I know myself.

Thanks, Samar.

I will not force you, our getting married is your call.

:)

It is strange but I truly believe him. I don't think any other girl in an arranged marriage has been given this choice. If I want to proceed, we will, but otherwise we won't and he will help me convince my parents without any complains. This is 'why' my answer can never be anything but a resounding 'yes'.

I don't know why he still doubts my decision. Most probably he is just being a gentleman, who wants to assure me that he will keep his word. That's nice of him and I appreciate this gesture.

The flight is announced. I immediately move towards the line. To my surprise, Kabir joins the same queue. He is travelling to Nagpur too!

It would be ironic, if he is travelling to Nagpur for Samar? The world is a small place. Kabir, if I remember correctly, has some connection with Nagpur. I hope not. I am trying to move on.

I arrive at my seat and there he is, once again, this time sitting next to me. I should have expected that! After all, my life can't move a step without a fight with him.

I take my seat and try to avoid him as much as possible, but I can't help noticing that he texts someone before shutting down his cell phone. My phone beeps as I send '*boarded*' text to Samar before I have to switch off my phone.

Samar has messaged.

Have a safe trip, bye.

DP— big heart

DS - Waiting for the big day.

It makes me feel strange. He trust himself but not me. He wants to be with me, but is ready to let me go if I wish. It's surprising, how did he know I was boarding the plane? The flight is an hour late and I hadn't messaged him. How is his timing so perfect?

My mind is plagued with questions and doubts. Having Kabir next to me, only encourage negative thoughts. I close my eyes and try to sleep, hoping to ignore him and avoid becoming paranoid, but there is something fishy going on, I can sense it. The only good thing is that he does not try to speak to me. I can't wait for the flight to land and to begin my new life.

Unfortunately, with Kabir beside me there is no chance of a peaceful journey. He is an irritating passenger for co- travellers and the crew. The minute he sits he will ask for a glass of water, again, and again, and again. He is one thirsty soul, who gets even thirstier while travelling. As he calls the flight attendant, I try to make her and my life easier by interrupting him.

"Hi, I need a…" Kabir starts to say and gets irritated when I say, "a glass of water, and please keep repeating for at least 5 times, and also could you please shift my seat."

They both look at me in amazement. She looks at Kabir and Kabir nods his head in approval to what I had said. She asks me curiously.

"You want to be shifted away from your husband, madam?"

"Husband? He isn't my husband."

"Sorry, Ma'am, I assumed you were married since you were concerned."

"Well, we aren't and I would appreciate a different seat if possible."

"Sorry, Ma'am, the flight is full."

Like a moron he interrupts. "Is there a rule that only women married to a guy can be concerned about him? Can't she generally be concerned about me?"

"Certainly, Sir," says the air hostess, as he winks at her, deliberately trying to making me feel like a fool.

I was not really happy with all that was going on, as I didn't want to spend the whole flight remembering the good and bad times we spent together. I don't want to remember the good times as I have moved on and I don't want to think of the bad times because I don't want to hold on to my grudge any more.

I shut my eyes and pretend to sleep. It was not possible to sleep but yes, a little entertainment with a little pretence was possible. I kept listening to Kabir's acts. Like a sincere schoolboy, he eats the food, finishes everything served to him, and ensures that he takes only all he could eat. He has still not changed. I used to ask him if he was trained in a military school and he would just laugh at my question.

He would say that he would talk about where he was brought up when he was confident about me. He would always treat me as an immature person. Being older doesn't automatically make you mature.

Between my mental rants, I kept praying to all the Gods I can possibly remember, to escape my present. Finally, I hear the answer to my prayers, we were about to land. I felt like I had escaped prison as I left the plane.

By the time I collected my bags at the luggage counter, I was calm and resigned to Mr Wrongs' presence. I think I would even cope with his presence at my wedding if he was a friend of Samar. I never hide anything from Samar and if he is friends with Kabir, then that is not my fault. All my close friends, including my 'friends for life' are coming to my wedding; Samar's friends should be equally welcome. I am not going to let Kabir's presence bother me.

When I go to collect my luggage, I see Kabir at the other end. I make sure that I was out of his sight, which ensures my peace of mind. However angry I get at him for the wrong he has done, it doesn't change the fact that any girl who marries him will be fortunate. He is not meant for me, but I have no regrets. May he soon get his Mrs. Right just like I have found my Mr Right.

****

As I walk towards the exit, I feel happy about my new life. I look at the gate and notice everyone has come to receive me, including Papa. I am so happy to see him looking healthy. Its days like this that makes me count my blessings and thank God for the lovely people in my life.

I head to them with a bright smile, each step a little quicker, as my excitement increases. This is the first time all of them have come to receive me. God is being really kind to me. As I try to walk faster, balancing my luggage becomes difficult and as usual I topple over. This is so embarrassing, I am so glad this has never happened at work. It would have given the management even more reasons to question my capability to be a VP.

After I pick myself, I come face to face with a shock of my life— the person whom I was avoiding is standing with my family. Did I hit my head? Do I have a concussion? Should I ask my family to take me to the hospital?

I pinch myself. No, this is real. Kabir is really standing amongst my family members. They are hugging him, as if they know him, as if he is a close family friend.

What the hell is going on? How does my family know Kabir? Why are they treating him like a member of the family?

I continue looking at them silently, until they notice me. Everyone becomes quiet and there was awkwardness in air. My brothers and Roma give me a quick hug, before Suraj rushes to call the driver and Shreyas to collect my bags. Roma starts talking to Kabir while my parents join me.

They are all acting funny and I am standing there like a mute, train-wrecked spectator. Finally, I manage to speak.

"Can someone please tell me what the hell is happening?"

I was irritated and frustrated. I felt cheated and backstabbed. I felt disgusted. I started crying at the airport, trying to demand answers.

"Have you broken off my marriage with Samar? Did he mention anything wrong about me? Papa, what's going on? How do you know Kabir? Why is he here?"

"Nisha, get into the car, I will explain everything once we get home."

"No, Papa, I am not entering the car, I want to know what is going on, right now."

Papa stares at me. Suraj says.

"Nisha, we are going home. Come, let's talk at home." I looked at him in disbelief. Why is he being like this?

Papa's look softens, "I understand your concern. I will explain at home. Please, let's get inside the car."

I couldn't understand what was happening. I wanted to leave, but this was my family. I needed to know everything... What I had done so terrible that they were treating me this way? I enter the car, but I decide to sit next to the driver. I needed the distance.

Despite my best efforts, tears kept rolling down my face and my family ignored me. Neither my mother nor my father tried to console me or explain. Suraj, Shreyas and Roma chose to drive with Kabir. I felt that I was the stranger not him. I had been treated better by colleagues, who hated me. I felt that I had no value in my house. Despite my concerns and doubts, I kept quiet until we entered the house.

As we step inside I ask Papa. "How do you know Kabir?"

Epilogue

"Nisha, he is Kabir Samar Singh."

"What?"

"Nisha, I need you to calm down. I know you are confused and have many questions. I will answer all of them, but you have to be quiet and listen to me."

"Papa, you want me to calm down? Are you serious?"

"Promise me that you will listen."

"Do I have any other option, Papa? I just feel like killing myself right away."

"Nisha."

"I promise to listen, but you need to start talking quickly. I feel like my family has plotted against me to get me to marry a man, whom I have despised for years. I feel like I don't know any of you and I don't belong to this family. At least at work, when people plot against you, it is expected. They are looking to secure or improve their positions. I never expected my family to plot against me because I trusted you."

"Nisha, don't overreact. You know that we all love you."

"I thought so until I landed!"

"Stop being so melodramatic, Nisha."

"I am human, Papa, I have the right to react to this shock of my life."

"Do you remember sending your mom a picture of you and Vikram, saying friends forever?"

"Yes, Papa, I remember, but that does not mean that it is OK for you to create a fake person for me to marry and trick me to marry the one person whom I hate the most in this world."

"Do you remember that she didn't call you for a few days after receiving that picture?"

"Papa, this discussion is about how you know Kabir and why you lied about Samar, not about Vikram. Why are you changing the subject?"

"Nisha, I will answer all of your questions, but I will do it my way. You agreed to listen. This is not listening. Now listen, else I don't have anything to say. Do you remember that your mom didn't call you for a few days after receiving the picture of you and Vikram?"

"Yes, Papa, of course I do. What is new about that? Mom always acts strange and overreacts when it comes to proposals."

"No, Nisha, she wasn't acting strange or overreacting. She was depressed. She was blaming herself."

"For what?"

"She believes that she is responsible for the delay in your marriage. She wanted you to have more than a mediocre life. She wanted more for you, than being a simple housewife. She encouraged you to study hard and have a career. She became depressed, thinking all her encouragement and advice ruined you, that you will live a cold and solitary life."

"Papa, that's not true."

"Nisha, just listen, don't interrupt," says Suraj interrupting and taking over, as he sees Papa getting stressed and me getting hyper.

They dropped Kabir to a hotel and rushed home, as Suraj bhai was aware that the situation at home would not be as easy to handle. He feels that his sister was not an easy animal to deal with and especially for our simple parents.

"Yes, Nisha, Mom had gone into a depression and we worked really hard to get her out of it."

"I didn't know that, Bhai."

"It's because we did not tell you, Nisha. There was no point since you were so lost in your own growth and career, that talking to you would have made no impact."

"Bhai, you could have mentioned that there is a problem, at least once. How do you know how I would react?"

"Nisha, Papa had complained about chest pain during that time and I went to Mumbai with him to meet the doctor while you were in Goa for your conference. It so happened that I bumped into Mr Bijal, who was visiting a friend at the same hospital. He is a really nice man. While we were talking, Mr Bijal mentioned Kabir."

"I was shocked. I remember us looking for the perfect

man for you around that time. I remember you meeting five or six of those prospects during the time and you didn't even say a word to us about Kabir. Who cheated whom Nisha—you or us? Papa was so upset at that time, you had already decided to go to the US and he had to reject those guys.

I was shocked and disappointed. I couldn't believe my little Nishu would do like this," said Suraj.

Nisha was in tears as her brother mentioned about what the family was going through while she was enjoying her comfortable life back in Mumbai. She felt guilty, but yes, she had a reason for all her actions. She didn't rise to this level just like that.

"Bhai, I didn't tell you about Kabir because I was so unsure about him, about our future together. Yes, I was madly in love with him, but there was something that always kept me quiet. Then I realised that we started fighting, which became all the more reason for me to not to tell you about him. I wasn't sure we would last and we actually didn't."

"I never asked you anything, Nisha, not even once. I trusted my sister."

"I am sorry I hurt everyone's feelings. I wasn't plotting against you or your desires. I just really liked him and then our relationship was over before it could get stronger. I am sorry, Bhai, Maa and Papa."

Nisha cried and begged all of them. She looked at Roma and saw her holding Dhara, as if to give her the confidence that all would be fine.

The only thing Suraj hated in life was to see tears in Nishas' eyes. He couldn't bear to see her cry, but this time he couldn't afford to be affected, to be swayed. No more tricks, no more games, everything was over, she had to be confronted. He got hold of himself and continued.

"Once I found out about the relationship, I asked Mr Bijal about Kabir. He told me about the argument and your need to prove yourself. He told me about Kabir, as a person. He is successful. He is genuinely a good person. Moreover, whatever he did was to get you out of the trouble, which you had unknowingly gotten into."

"Trouble?"

"That's a discussion you need to have with Kabir.

Kabir hadn't settled down either... He even has ties with Nagpur through his mother. So, I got details about his family, I personally went to meet his mother and shared my concerns. She is a very nice person. She, just like Mom, was worried that her son would never settle down and she was happy to know about both of you. She called up Kabir and asked him to come home immediately. We got to know the real story from him."

Despite knowing everything, Suraj believed that whatever happens would be at Nisha's will. He did not mention anything about it to the family trying to cover-up for Nisha, as always. But when his father had a stroke, he realised some things had to be mended. He wanted to get everything on track without letting anyone know. If in the bargain his relationship with his little sister gets sour then so be it. She is not always right.

Mr Chandra broke the silence with his words. They were informed about everything very late.

"Nisha, the misunderstanding between the two of you comes down to ego. You need to be the best. This is not completely your fault. You and your brothers are self-centred at times, because we encouraged ambition, and forgot to teach you about humility. It was only when Suraj told us about Kabir that we understood the whole story. Nisha, why would Suraj refuse to send us to you for my health and our family happiness? All he wanted was to get to the root cause of the situation and fix the problem."

As he talked to Nisha, who was in tears and listening to him like a little girl, he put his hand on her head, making her comfortable.

"As of Kabir, Kabir is a gem of a person, Nisha. The two of you grew closer as you spoke via messages. He didn't even have to lie about his background. It's funny the two of you were so close, but you didn't know about his roots to your own city, nor did you know his family background or his full name. I am amazed at the way this generation talks about love and relationship, like a blind bunch of people."

He looks at her with warmth in his eyes.

"Nisha, you liked Samar, didn't you? A fresh, faceless meeting without any preconceptions of who he is or how he will affect your career. Did you like the person who you were talking to?"

"Yes, but..." she begins and her father interrupts.

"But nothing. After we met him, all of us were of the opinion that a fresh meeting would change your mind. This was easy to achieve once you decided not to meet your fiancé face to face until the day of the wedding.

You found about Kabir today, because four days ago, Kabir called to tell us that he wasn't sure you felt anything except hatred for him. He felt it would be unfair to spring his presence on you just before the wedding ceremony. We decided the two of you would fly together, to give you a chance to talk and clear the air. But coming together, yet not talking, gave us a clear picture of what transpired.

The decision is now yours. Kabir has asked us to inform that you still have tonight to think. If your answer is yes, then we will proceed with the ring ceremony, but if you still feel that you hate him then you may say no, and he will silently step back without a word.

You need to decide. If you love him, this is your final chance with him. If you decide not to marry him, then we will stop looking for the perfect groom and we will ignore what society says. Your life is your own."

"Papa, have you said all you needed to say?"

"Yes."

"Now can I say something? Do I have the right?"

"Nisha, you have the right to say what you want and you have the right to live your life the way you want. We don't have any issues with that. The only thing that hurt us and will always hurt us, whether you marry Samar or not, is that you never said anything about him to us."

She looks at her father and speaks.

"Papa, I tried to explain earlier. Why don't you understand? I liked Kabir but he was such a difficult person that I was unsure of my choice. I was going to tell you about him when you came along with Mom to meet that prospect Rahul but just before you arrived Kabir and I fought and we broke up. I was upset and took my ill temper out on Rahul, refusing to even give him a chance to talk about himself.

I agree, I should have told you what had happened. I don't know what Kabir has informed you about our relationship but I want to tell you about what transpired.

I met Kabir on my very first day at the Bijal Group. Our paths crossed even before I entered the office. He was driving towards the parking while I was hurrying towards the lift. I crossed in front of his car and he yelled at me very badly. I entered the office and I was asked to wait in a small conference room for the Manager of Operations, my reporting head. He entered and I was mortified. Our first meeting was bad, he was irritated and I was extremely nervous.

He looked at me sternly and asked, "Are you sure you want to build your career, Ms Nisha?"

I looked at him, a little confused, and replied, "I have been working towards a career since I was in 11th standard."

"That's a good answer, but keep in mind that our work

demands more than a conversation or being a recipient of Mr Bijal's number game. I expect you to perform right from the start and failure to perform will require you to look for another job. So, carefully consider whether or not you are serious about this job before we begin today."

I kept quiet for a little while and then he packed me off with a junior from his department. The colleague that showed me around, had worked with Kabir for a few years and showered him praise. He said that he was a brilliant man from whom I could learn a lot. He said the department under Kabir was the gateway to the core department. He was known to groom people with the right skill set and dedication. Unfortunately, if he disapproves a person, he rarely has a future within the group. He also warned me that I should watch out for his temper and ego, as even Mr Bijal kept silent when Kabir loses his temper.

As I began to work with him, I realised that Kabir was brilliant, but many people simply agreed with his decisions, because they wanted to remain in his good books. We began clashing at work when I started questioning his judgments. Initially things were bad, but later the situation improved as he realised my reasoning was sound. We still fought, but we worked together more easily.

Six months after we started working together, out of the blue, he asked me out. I didn't know how to react. I wasn't a close friend like Ms Priya or Shrija nor did we have the most comfortable relationship. I didn't know what to do so I ignored the proposal.

I became close to Shrija due to this proposal. He had discussed his feelings for me with Shrija, and she came up to me to discuss whether I had feelings for him. I told her that the person whom I marry was not up to me. My parents would decide and if anyone had feelings or was serious about the proposal, then he should speak to my parents. I don't know how he took the message.

Even my friend Kiran noticed that Kabir's behaviour had become very strange. As the days passed, Kabir and my working relationship began to deteriorate. He would snap at me over little things. I decided, either I needed to find another job or register a complaint with HR. I couldn't handle the ill-treatment. That day as I left, he stopped me and asked for an answer. I informed him that he would have to talk to you. We fought that day. Both of us made nasty comments. He called me a narrow-minded, small-town girl and I called him a power- hungry chauvinist. I wanted nothing to do with him.

I changed my mind later due to Shrija and mom. Shrija laughed when I told her about the fight and said that Kabir is a good guy and I should give him a chance. I spoke to Mom, later that day without giving the any background about Kabir, we had a general conversation like usual. She said that if I ever come across someone whom I wanted to marry, then I must tell you, but I must be thoroughly sure that he would keep me happy all my life.

I kept Mom's and Shri's words in mind and decided to speak to Kabir about his proposal. When I spoke to him, he told me that he was talking about marriage and not just a casual relationship. He said that he had clearly stated that he wanted to be with me for life and not less. He told me if I was interested then he had no problem in meeting with you, but if I wasn't interested in him there was no point in wasting time. He said as far as work is concerned, I still needed improvement. He was also very clear that work is work and personal life is personal life. He told me that he liked me because I was different from the other girls, that I had self-respect, decency and fearlessness.

I asked him if we could see how it goes for some time and if all is well then I would like him to meet you, Papa, we did give the relationship some time, but his attitude irritated me. At work, he was one person and when we would meet personally he was someone else. I could not take his dual personality, this led to a number of arguments, he tried to prove his point of view and I tried to prove mine. He would yell at small, small things and I tolerated a lot. When Kiran left, she warned me against Kabir, she told me that he was making all the efforts to remove me from the system. He wanted me to sit at home and become a housewife. I don't know why he wanted that and why was it known to Kiran and not me.

During the time we were together, Papa, I informed you I had a very heavy workload and could not meet anyone. Around that time, I decided to speak to you, but he created such a huge scene at the office that it caused me to change my mind. Six safety helmets from the same batch were rejected, but the report of the batch did not indicate this failure. I mailed all concerned people to understand, where the error was generated, but he blamed me for the mistake. It turned out the line manager forced a worker to work for 18 hours, which was against the mandate since there was a shortage of manpower and this led to the blunder.

This incident made me realise that he did not think I was good enough. I decided to resign, and take up the offer from the US company, but Shrija changed my mind. She convinced me to speak to Mr Bijal and HR and switch department instead. I was hurt and embarrassed about the situation so I didn't tell you anything when you came to visit. Once you had gone, I switched department and dedicated my time to proving my worth and I promised myself that one day I would become a VP.

So, Papa, this is the whole story, I don't know what version he told you, but for me he does not exist at all. I don't know how to play a game with the same person in two courts."

There was a silence again; the daughter of the family was giving an explanation of - 'why she did not disclose her relationship'. We all stay in a society that has its own parameters for the face value of it, but underneath is a web of complicated lives struggling to find their own reasons of existence. Nisha was not sure of what she did wrong nor were her parents sure of what to blame her for, neither the guy was refusing marriage, nor did she intend to have a short-term fling with him. Even the parents were out of the narrow-minded society parameters. Still there was a silence.

Her brother looked at her beloved sister and finally said.

"Nisha, we don't have anything against you. All we want is your happiness, but if you had mentioned to us just once about this person we could have tried to resolve the issue."

"Bhai, the issue is his hypocrisy and chauvinism. When you knew the whole story, why did you not come to me? Why did you have to go to him? What was the point in believing him more than me? Had you asked me, I would have told you. I have been carrying this burden for such a long time."

"What did you find in Samar that you don't see in Kabir?"

"Bhai, please don't try to twist the question. Why did you not come to me?"

"Nisha, I am not trying to twist anything, I am just trying to understand the situation."

"Bhai, it just means that you don't trust your own sister."

"Honestly, Nisha, when you plotted your exit from Nagpur to Mumbai eight years ago, you lost our complete and blind trust. That might sound hurtful, but yes, we had doubts. We didn't think you would do anything wrong, but we were aware that you are capable of twisting the truth to suit yourself."

Nisha looks at her brother, and entire family. She knows the mistake she has made and is apologetic. She is their framed culprit, not Kabir. She had to somehow

tackle this situation and get to the actual culprit. Still unaware of the goof-up that Kiran had created, she was thinking of how to meet Kabir and give him her piece of mind. She continued to tell them, her version of the story.

"Bhai, over the SMS conversation, Samar would talk just like Kabir used to outside the office. This is the reason that I felt I knew him. What I failed to realise was that my own brother had teamed up with him to play a trick against me. You made it so difficult for me. You played a game against me. You used Papa's health as a plot to blackmail me. Bhai, what do you think you would have got out of all this? Is it marriage with Roma? Bhai, I never stopped you from going ahead. Why should you spoil a girl's life because your family is not capable of resolving its own internal issues? The Chandra's as a family can't even decide whether we want to go by social norms or carve our own path."

Her volume started rising and hearing that Suraj tried to control her.

"Listen, Nisha, lower your voice, Papa has still not recovered. And as far as Roma and my marriage is concerned, we don't need your permission. We are not fools like you. We understand each other. She is my life partner; I would never leave her. I'm not an idiot like you. Kabir was trying to be sensible and understanding while resolving the mess that your best friend Kiran had got you into. She purposely poisoned your mind, making things difficult for Kabir, while making false transactions in your name that would destroy your career and your reputation.

Our parents never taught us to distrust anyone but you failed to trust yourself, Nishu. He is a nice man and you can trust your brother on this. If you still feel we are all plotting against you, by getting you married to Mr Wrong and getting rid of our responsibilities, then you should check with Mr Bijal. He promised Kabir that the topic would never crop up and you would never know what your best friend had done behind your back. He did not want your confidence destroyed. He respects you, he didn't want to see you break?

Nisha, you like the man he was outside of work. You didn't like the persona at work because he is a very practical person. The fact that he is a different person at work is not wrong as his work demanded something more. And that position demanded much more. You have to balance between the two. You can't be the same kind of person you are at home, while at work as there is peoples' money involved. Trusting an emotional fool with responsibility is a huge risk. When Kabir explained this to you, you got offended, but when Samar tried to explain the same logic to you, you understood it perfectly. Why? It was only because of the perceptions you hold on to.

Trust me, Nisha, I don't know how much influence Kiran's words have on your perception of Kabir, but if it does then you are not the right person for Kabir. He is much above your thinking."

"Bhai, I don't think even now that I know Kabir," I say.

"I think you should talk to him, Nisha, and if you still feel he is wrong then, we leave it up to you."

With these last words, Nisha was left by herself. She tossed and turned, the whole night long trying to decide which path to take.

After all the arguments, meeting Kabir is pointless. It will only lead to more pain. Maybe I should call up Vikram and ask him to marry me. My parents will be happy and I know Vikram is a gentleman. I will be happy with him.

It wasn't anything else, but her ego, that was not letting her give in. She did not want to believe Suraj despite knowing he was right. She was proving the ancient saying - ego is self-destructive. Kiran had no role to play in her life anymore, but she is considered as a reason to have changed her life completely. Nisha could have been a housewife and a mother of two kids, had it not been for that incident that changed her life.

Vikram has been just a friend but he could become her husband. In the fight of proving herself right, Nisha was just giving in and giving into any and everything thing right or wrong.

****

The next day, surprisingly, no one behaved strangely or even asked her for her decision. Roma only asked her if she wanted to meet Samar.

She agreed, wanting to give him a piece of her mind, for plotting with the family. They meant well, but who knows what his end game is in this plot.

The meeting was arranged. He came home. Her family left them alone. The meeting was awkward but she wanted answers from him.

With anger in her eyes, she looked at him, it's not the first time he has seen this anger, but he had no energy left to handle it. He still did not want to give up, he wanted to be with her, but he was scared - what if it did not work out? It would be all over.

She saw him, stared at him, continued to stare at him and then there was a loud clap of a slap, which broke the vocal silence of six years. Yes, she slapped him, but no one came in and dared to interfere in the matter of the confused couple.

"How dare you, Kabir? How dare you? Who gave you the right to play with my feelings and my family's feelings?"

Kabir never expected this out of his lady love. He looked at her shocked as she continued.

"Kabir, I never expected all this from you, my parents are simple people and you plotted against me with them."

It was for the first time Nisha had ever slapped him. No, she was not happy about it, she was rather shivering. She was not sure of Kabir's reaction, he could hit her back, but if he did that, she would not get even a second to feel the shock; his slap would collapse her on the spot. But he did not react. He was composed, he knew what she meant, he knew what he could have done and what the fear of her unpredictable emotions made him do.

"Nisha, this wasn't a plot or a game. I just wanted to break you away from your rigid thinking. You couldn't deal with my role at work and that affected our personal life. We began fighting needlessly. Our lives became a competition. Every argument at work marked me as evil in your mind. I couldn't get you to change your mind and we parted ways. I still had feelings for you, but I decided to move on. I never met another person who felt as right as you. So, when your brother approached my mother and we started talking about our relationship, I expressed that I wanted another chance. But I was sure you wouldn't even consider it if your brother directly approached you about me. I had tried doing that through the *shaadi* portal once, but you slammed it without even considering. I strongly believe that relationships are made in heaven and that is the only reason why we still are not able to move on. All we needed was a fresh start, and this plot was a chance at a fresh start."

"So you admit you were behind the plot, Kabir?"

"Yes, I helped come up with the plan, but our only goal was to set up a fresh, bias-free meeting between you and me."

"Bias-free? How is it bias-free if one person knows and the other doesn't? You even had access to my family to ensure that your replies suited the occasion perfectly. Kabir, you could have come and told me about Kiran yourself, I am not mad to not believe you. Why did you not do that? Do you even realise that you have taken six years of my damn life?"

"Nisha, I have lost those years too."

"Kabir, what about my family? What wrong have they done to you? Had you clarified to me back then there would have been no need for this stupid game that you played. What is the need to complicate things, Kabir? I was there for you, I decided to leave my job in order to settle with you but you played with my life? How dare you think of my life as a video game?"

"I always tried to find opportunities to talk to you, but you never allowed me."

"How could I—you fool, it was you who told me that I wasn't good at work and I better sit at home, how could I stand you in the office then?"

"I told you the reason behind it, Nisha, it was only because I cared for you."

"Kabir, you cared so much that you got my family and me into this mess."

"I never knew how to tell you and I have suffered for that all these years."

"You deliberately invited me for the dinner and next day planted the rose decoration both in the office and at my flat with the same contractor. You got Karishma remarried to her husband. Wherever you failed in striking a chord as Kabir, you tried fixing it as Samar. You knew the entire game, you got my family to your side, you knew they would listen to your story and agree to the proposal, and you knew that at the end of the game, only you would win. Like a fool I kept wondering about what was happening around me and you happily took advantage of my innocence."

"Nisha, now you are going overboard, what advantage have I taken? This marriage is still at your mercy. If you say 'no', nothing will move forward and not even a single person will say a word."

"Oh really, Kabir, there are cards printed, leaves sanctioned, guests coming, you have trapped me and now you ask me—how have you taken advantage of me?"

"Nisha, are you sure I took advantage of your innocence? There were people who have already done that, do you even know what had happened in the past?"

"I have been briefed about the Kiran story and I am sure even that is a cooked-up story. You could have come to me directly and spoken about it, right? Why did you have to create a fake identity to talk to me? I really wonder, Kabir, if you are the person whom I loved."

She went on and on…he steps closer and puts his hand over her mouth to make her stop and listen.

"Nisha, Kiran, your best friend was doing illegal transactions in your name without your notice."

"I don't believe you Kabir."

"Nisha tell me after Kiran's exit interview did HR not ask you about your account details?"

"Meaning?"

"Meaning – they wanted to see your transaction details and confirm if there was any fraud. And there were two-three instances when some money had been transferred from Kiran's account to yours."

"But that was my money which she used to borrow at the time of need and return once she had."

"Why did she do a bank transaction? She could have removed from ATM and handed over the money to you, just like how you would give to her. You never gave her cheques or went to the bank to deposit money in her account."

"That is because she insisted....."

"Exactly that is the whole point. And in one single month she deliberately did that twice."

"I don't even remember the exact details."

"That is because you never cared for what was happening in the background. You just blindly trusted her. Nisha your reputation was at stake and had I made a slight mistake things could have gotten worse."

"But Kabir you could have told me...."

"Nisha trust me everything that I did, I did for us, and I did not want to see you hurt. My mother single-handedly raised me. She took charge of our two-member family when my father left her to suffer. She always wanted to be a social worker and help the underprivileged without realising that one day she would be left to support her own family. She was the man of our house. I watched her suffer and couldn't do anything to help her. It was then I decided that I would never leave the woman I love to suffer for anything. Your passion for work was good, but the situation you were in would have harmed you terribly. I tried to fix that without you knowing. I tried to offer you a life away from work. Do you know that I bought a sea-facing home for us? I was going to show you the night you broke up with me. I loved you, but I let you go because I knew I could never let you suffer. If you want to grow in the career, you would grow. The time when my mother had to struggle was different, but today time is different. You never suffered, you only grew, and you were prepared for all the challenges unlike Mother. And I was there to guard you from the backstage. I realised your strength much later, but by then you were lost in your passion to become a VP. Nisha, I respect you for who you are."

She listened to him quietly. He had never really opened up to her before. She finally understood the reason behind some of his actions. If only he had spoken to her before, maybe they wouldn't have broken up.

She is nudged out of her thoughts as he continues.

"Nisha, I didn't need help talking to you. I needed help getting through those metre-high fences you built. Your family only set-up the SMS conversation, they did not help me write any messages."

"Yes, and I am supposed to believe that?"

"Yes, Nisha. See, this is the problem. You get an idea fixed in your head and you will not listen to reason. You will not listen to explanations. Life, work and personal, requires communication to succeed. You want people to listen to you, but you are not prepared to listen."

"You have an answer to everything, Kabir. Of course, I am still an incompetent fool who took eight years to become a VP while you were made one much much earlier. You definitely have charm, otherwise why would Mr Bijal in every meeting suggest that I take grooming tips from you," I growl at him.

"I don't know anything between you and Bijal Sir. All I know is that I love you, Nisha."

"If you feel like that, then why plot and plan and ruin my relationship with my family."

"Why don't you have a good relationship with your family? Why do they trust a stranger more than their own daughter? I am sure you know the reason better. Listen, I still like the person you are inside despite your stubbornness. As for your relationship with your family, I am not responsible. I wanted to meet your family all those years ago, you were the one who wanted to wait. They are disappointed. Trust me years of frustration and drama could have been avoided if you had said a single word about meeting someone."

"Yes. Sure."

"Nisha, they would have never found out about me if you hadn't upset your mother with that picture of Vikram. Your dad and brother wouldn't have travelled to Mumbai, bumped into Mr Bijal and learnt of our relationship. You cannot blame me for that! You need to take responsibility for your actions."

"Fine, I will. Since my picture was the cause of this drama, I will call up Vikram and ask him to marry me. Problem solved. My parents will be happy I will get